don't

EXPLAIN

Other books by the author:

Oral Tradition
Forty-Three Septembers
The Gilda Stories
Flamingoes and Bears
The Lipstick Papers

don't
EXPLAIN

short fiction by

JEWELLE GOMEZ

Firebrand
Books
Ithaca, New York

Earlier versions of several of these stories have appeared in the following books and periodicals: *On Our Backs, Oxford World Treasury of Love Stories, Penguin Book of Lesbian Short Stories, Serious Pleasures, Sisterfire, Swords of the Rainbow,* and *Zyzzyva.*

"Don't Explain," words and music by Arthur Herzog, Jr., and Billie Holiday
"Water with the Wine," words and music by Joan Armatrading

Book and cover design by Nightwood

Printed in Canada

10 9 8 7 6 5 4 3 2 1

Library of Congress Cataloging-in-Publication Data

Gomez, Jewelle, 1948—
    Don't explain : short fiction / by Jewelle Gomez.
        p.   cm.
    Contents: White flower—Don't explain—Grace A.—Steps—Ounce of charm—Water with the wine—Piece of time—Lynx and strand—Houston.
    ISBN 1-56341-095-8 (cloth : alk. paper). —ISBN 1-56341-094-x (pbk. : alk. paper)
    I. United States—Social life and customs—Fiction. 2. Afro-American women—Fiction. I. Title.
  PS3557.0457D66   1998
  813'.54—dc21   98-15781
                                                                       CIP

Grateful thanks go to:

Nancy Bereano, Linda Nelson, Cheryl Clarke, David Dietcher, Dorothy Allison, Urban Bush Women—past, present, and future— Maria Lachina who I will miss always, the generous-hearted women in my writing workshops at BRAVA!, Mama Bears Books, J.C. Collins, Alexis DeVeaux (whose wonderful book of the same title inspired my story), Albert Friedman, Mad Dog of S.F., Marianne, Sandra, Irene, and Elaine and the many women of our generation who are still trying to survive their families. And Diane Sabin.

Chap 3

My work is dedicated to Gracias Archelina Sportsman Morandus, Lydia M. Morandus, John J. Gomes.

CONTENTS

WHITE FLOWER

Luisa picked up the ringing telephone absent-mindedly, tucking it between her shoulder and ear while she signed the shipping invoice. "Sportswear on Four," she said. Three beats of silence on the other end made Luisa flush with warmth and wave her co-worker away.

"May I help you?" she said crisply, knowing what the response would be.

"Yes, White Flower, you can."

"When?" Luisa's voice was dry and even, although her heart raced. Her nylons began to feel scratchy on her legs, her skin prickled with excitement.

"Tuesday."

She smiled. I guess Belmont Park is still closed on Tuesdays, she thought, remembering how it had been when they first met the year before. Between swimming, yoga, volunteer night, working late, department meetings, and, of course, the racetrack, there had been little time to have even a first date. Tuesday always turned out to be the best bet.

"Yes," Luisa said. "Tuesday, 6:30. I'll come up."

[handwritten margin note, right side:] over-achieving protagonist

[handwritten margin note, bottom:] Why does she have to always be Made into an over achiever

That would give them twelve hours.

"Good," came the throaty response. It was deep, musical, but hard at the edges. "It's been a long time. See you then." Click.

Luisa hung up the receiver. Her palms were sweating. Her silk blouse stuck to her back, in spite of the cool air circulating from the department store air-conditioning system. The white carnation, identifying her as a floor manager, was crisp in her lapel. Sometimes she wore the artificial flower the store supplied, but Luisa preferred a fresh carnation and its cinnamon scent. She held onto the desk and tried to catch her breath. It had been two months since the last time; she could make it until Tuesday, surely.

A saleswoman broke into Luisa's disguised hysteria. "Lu, this guy is driving me nuts. He keeps—"

"It's okay, I'll talk to him," she answered with a smile at the red-haired girl, who looked relieved. Everyone hated to get involved in prolonged disagreements with customers just before closing time, particularly on a Saturday night. But any distraction from the wave of excitement which threatened to envelope her suited Luisa fine. She patted her forehead and nose with a paper towel, her aunt's voice in her head: "Try not to be shiny when you talk to white people, it makes them nervous." She pushed the stockroom's swinging doors and went out onto the sales floor.

Super woman again

Later, the customer appeased, Luisa changed into the walking shoes she kept in her locker and said good night to the women remaining behind to tally the registers. She took the downtown train, determined to avoid going home until as late as possible. That would mean one more night had passed, bringing her closer to Tuesday.

Luisa came up out of the subway, relieved to feel the cooler air in the square, and crossed against the traffic. She was anxious to be inside the refuge of the Club. The rush of people was invigorating; even dodging taxi cabs made her laugh as she darted for the Club's front door. She didn't glance around until she was served a gin and tonic. Resting her chin on her hands, she listened to the music from the jukebox with her eyes closed. She was plotting how to occupy her Sunday and Monday evenings when she felt a hand on her thigh. She opened her eyes slowly.

"Damn! I could've had all your stuff and gone, as slow as you are!" Then came a booming laugh as a perfectly manicured, plump hand squeezed Luisa's leg.

"I thought you'd be on vacation," Luisa said, surprised.

"Naw, this year I'm going away in August, like the shrinks." Donna's laughter made her blues eyes sparkle and her light brown curls shake all around her head.

Whenever Luisa ran into Donna they ended up spending the evening catching up with each other's news between dances. Donna's Bronx edge overwhelmed some, but Luisa loved her raw energy. Her arrival was a good-luck sign to Luisa. She ordered another gin and tonic and a club soda for Donna.

"Sober and smiling, three years." Donna raised her glass.

"Congratulations!" Luisa said, toasting Donna.

When the woman next to Luisa moved, Donna climbed onto the bar stool. She was a large woman, tall and broad. "Built like a prison matron," she would sometimes say with a leer. The image seemed incongruous given the delicate reality of her. Her size, the passionate curl of her mouth, and her wit were all inviting, not forbidding. The two women drank a little, danced until they were both out of breath.

"Well, we've got a date next week," Luisa said tentatively, trying to hold her enthusiasm in check.

Donna didn't comment. She continued to look at the bubbles making their way to the top of her glass of soda.

"It's been like this for a year. We can't have a relationship. We've tried, and it makes us both crazy. It's too consuming, too everything. But when we try to stay apart I feel like something died inside." Luisa plucked the wilted carnation from her lapel and tossed it onto the bar.

"Can I say something?" Donna's usually bright look was subdued. Her tone stopped Luisa's picking at the discarded flower.

"I don't want to talk out of turn, Lu. I think a lot of you, you know. But this is a fly-by-night kind of thing." Donna sighed as if she'd been holding in the statement for too long.

"This is how it works best for us."

"Lu, this is how it works best for who? Not you!"

Luisa picked up her glass and put it down, then played with the little paper napkin before she spoke.

"What do you know about it, Donna?"

"Just what you tell me."

Luisa closed up.

"Hey, you make your own choices, Lu. But please, if you don't mind being dangled on a string, at least think about safety."

"Safety?" Luisa snorted. "God, Donna, next you'll be passing out dental dams, or some other white girl shit!"

"I would if I had one."

The music was steady around them but did not fill the space. Luisa sipped from her glass.

"I'm only saying—" Donna stopped as Luisa set her glass down on the bar too firmly. She went on, "You know better than I do, but I get the feeling every time you talk about the whole affair, you're only talking about your side of the story."

"What's that mean?"

"You've been seeing each other, what, a year? From week to week you never know when you're going to have a date. Then your number turns up again, heaven for one night, then BANG, you're on your own. It's like you forget how miserable you were, until the next time. Then romance and melodrama all over again. Why?"

"We agreed not to make a deal out of it."

"I know you agreed, but why?"

Luisa pulled a few bills from her purse and pushed her stool back. "Look, I'll see you later."

Donna jumped down from her stool. "Yeah, see you, maybe Friday?"

Luisa returned Donna's look of anxiety with a half-smile, then walked toward the front door.

She filled Sunday with laundry, paying bills, swimming, and a call home to her aunt in Baltimore. She mopped the floor, pressed clothes, and decided what to wear for the rest of the week, beginning and ending with Tuesday. Luisa kept Donna's words pushed to the back of her mind and ignored them as she made her way through the hours. She played with her cat, then rented two movies which she watched back-to-back, only pausing to prepare dinner.

As she stirred the rice and turned the chicken she tried, for the first time, to imagine the others. Although she knew they existed,

the others.
who?

she couldn't see their faces. The one or two times in public when the opportunity had presented itself, Luisa had quickly turned away as if the other women were apparitions who only became real if she looked.

Luisa arrived at the store early on Monday. She checked the new shipment of jackets in the stockroom, made up marking instructions before most of the floor personnel had arrived, then went upstairs to the cafeteria for coffee. She had only one cup. The muscles across her shoulders already felt as taut as guitar strings, and it was too long a day for burnout. She vowed to have something soothing for dinner. Like a martini.

drinking issue again

That night Luisa went to the gym, then came home and watched television and read simultaneously. She fell asleep easily after the eleven o'clock news but awoke abruptly several hours later. She was accustomed to these waves of anticipation. Tonight, though, they chilled her. She pulled the extra blanket up from the foot of the bed and burrowed under all the covers.

It was barely light on Tuesday when she rose. Luisa wanted to give herself time to be sure she was satisfied with wearing the soft cotton pants and bright blouse she had laid out. She peered at herself in the full-length mirror in her tiny bathroom and was pleased. Her brown skin had a sheen under the coconut oil. Her eyes were alive and inviting. Donna's question popped into her mind: *Why?* She slipped a vial of rose oil into her purse.

It turned out to be the kind of day that left everyone frazzled: an overflow of irate customers, a shortage of staff, an excess of snippy managers—all on a sale day. Luisa maintained a small smile through it all. Her clothes stayed crisp, her feet didn't even hurt.

When she emerged from the employee ladies' room at 5:30, her make-up was light and perfect. She looked as fresh as she had in the morning. Luisa walked to the Sixth Avenue bus. Relieved to get a window seat, she stared out at the crowded street. Ever since she had moved up from Baltimore the melange of people on the city streets had invigorated her. The energy bouncing around her was like fuel. She loved the crowded library where she met the young woman she tutored every Thursday. Waiting on line to pay for her vegetables at the Korean grocery always turned into a social event. Sitting in the

Why did Gomez choose to put her as a store Manager

oh comon!

bar, even when she didn't want to drink, made her happy. Lively people moving around her were the reason she'd left home.

Luisa got off the bus on Riverside Drive. At precisely 6:30 she rang the doorbell and strode toward the elevator.

Upstairs, on the fourteenth floor, the apartment door opened just as Luisa stepped off the elevator. Naomi's smile was brilliant; her white teeth glistened. Her skin, almost the same shade as Luisa's, was smooth as velvet. The angled cut of her softly straightened hair swayed along the line of her cheekbones. The firmness of her bearing made her appear tall as she stepped back from the door and Luisa entered. Naomi wore white jeans, snug across her full thighs, and a large tailored shirt which swirled in a teasing way around her broad shoulders and small breasts. Only a slight trembling of her lips revealed her excitement.

Luisa watched Naomi watching her for a moment as if to be sure nothing had changed since they'd seen each other last. Then Naomi pulled Luisa inside the front door and into her arms, kissing her neck and cheek. Her body pushed forward, pressing Luisa backward, and she moved her leg between Luisa's as if it could enter her.

The smells of coconut oil and roses filled the air. She grabbed Luisa's hair, pulled her head back, and pushed her tongue deep into Luisa's mouth. The world dropped away as Luisa arched her back from the hard wood of the door to press more closely. Her hips moved in tight rhythm against Naomi's leg and the demanding pulse of Naomi's body drowned out Donna's questions. Luisa came softly, unable to stop herself.

Naomi asked, "Would you like a shower? I'd meant to say that first."

She watched as Luisa took off her clothes and stepped into the steamy stream of water. She sat on the toilet seat observing Luisa lather the soap. The tight bubbles slipped around the deep curve of her butt and turned in on her thigh.

Naomi reached in to catch the next spray of suds as they glistened on Luisa's belly. Luisa rinsed the soap off and waited. Naomi sat silently, gazing at Luisa's body for as long as she could. Luisa felt the other woman taking in her heavy breasts and brown nipples, the plump arms, the thick, curly pubic hair, the enticing curve of her calf. Luisa watched Naomi's breath quicken as if she could feel the texture of Luisa's skin by simply looking it over.

Luisa didn't fidget. She stared ahead, feeling Naomi's gaze as it slid over her skin. Naomi then draped a thick towel around Luisa's shoulders and rubbed her back, neck, and feet, every part roughly, lovingly. She led Luisa into the bedroom.

As usual, the large vase on the dresser was thick with white carnations. Luisa wondered fleetingly if Naomi always had them or if they were just for her. The blond wood of the bed stood out starkly against the dark blue and red African cloth that covered it.

Naomi and Luisa lay crosswise on the bed, as if thrown down to catch their breath. Luisa sat up on her arm to look again at this woman she knew and didn't know. They'd met when Naomi had asked Luisa's help buying a gift for a friend. Luisa had helped her pick out a soft sweater set and had restrained her curiosity. The next day, when Luisa saw Naomi get off the escalator, she knew Naomi had come back to see her.

After a few moments Luisa said, "Okay, what's the news? Don't leave me hanging. Did you get it or what?" → why does she start w/ this?

They picked up their conversation as if it had been hours since they'd been together instead of weeks. Yes, Naomi had bought her parents a video camera for their anniversary. The guy who was so much trouble had dropped out of the accounting class she taught.

Luisa was up to twenty laps and yoga twice a week. She'd made new curtains for her bedroom, helped to organize a demonstration at City Hall, and had seen almost every movie Naomi had.

But she never got to tell her. Naomi covered Luisa's mouth with her own, then pulled away to catch her breath. Luisa moved her hands from behind her head and started to caress Naomi. Instead, Naomi caught her hands and held them back at the edge of the bed. She clutched Luisa's wrists in one hand and ground her hips into her. The soft moans coming from both of them rose.

YUCK my pet peeve!

An hour later, Naomi slowly got up. Luisa arranged the pillows under her head.

"I better feed you, or you'll complain that I starve you." Naomi's smile was inscrutable as she grabbed her shirt from the floor and

like their relationship → sexually feeds her

FOOD = SEX

disappeared out the bedroom door. Her voice sounded as prim and hushed as a librarian's. There was a formality about her that was more intimate than nakedness.

She returned with a tray of food and a bottle of Merlot. They nibbled on bites of chicken pasta salad, made from Naomi's special recipe, while they talked about movies and gossiped.

"I think I'll always be yours," Luisa said bluntly.

Naomi's smile was dazzling and silent.

Luisa touched Naomi's mouth with the tip of her finger, smearing the oil caught in the corner. Moving the tray from the bed to the floor, she climbed on top of Naomi, tugging at the buttons of the large cotton shirt. She nuzzled Naomi's small breasts through the yielding material. Luisa wondered, again, how it was possible to hunger for someone she knew so little.

Her eyes widened in surprise: the enormity of desire was the only certainty between them. Their lovemaking was slow now, and Luisa forced the sound of Donna's question out of her head until they lay still in each other's arms.

"Do you want to watch the evening news?" Luisa asked, to keep from asking anything else.

"There is no evening. There is no news."

They lay exhausted as late night filled the room. Naomi pulled the sheet up to cover them and they slept.

Luisa woke on her stomach. She felt Naomi balancing herself lightly above her, brushing against her back. She matched the rhythm.

When Naomi felt the movement she pressed downward against Luisa. Luisa felt Naomi's body burn against hers as she pushed upward to meet Naomi's quickened movement.

It happened so fast, Luisa wasn't certain Naomi had come. She knew when she felt Naomi spread her legs apart and heard her say, "Up!" Luisa raised her ass high while Naomi continued to move against her, then her fingers entered Luisa from the rear. She opened wider and began the rocking motion that would cause the explosion. Naomi's voice, low above her ear, told her how much she needed her. Luisa rocked back and forth on Naomi's magic.

"Now, now, now," Naomi whispered, making Luisa's body shudder with release. They collapsed on the bed, trembling.

"That was beautiful," Naomi said. Luisa didn't answer as Naomi wrapped her arms around her. Within minutes both were deeply asleep.

Luisa woke before the alarm went off at 6:30 A.M., leaned over the bed and turned off the clock radio. As she listened to the sounds of morning outside and to Naomi's even breathing, the air was suddenly too close, too quiet inside. She hurried into her clothes while Naomi was still held by sleep, backed out of the room, and moved to the front door. She glanced back over her shoulder into the living room where she'd left the white silk scarf she'd bought for Naomi from First Floor Accessories.

She was back in her own apartment within half an hour. She *ritual* stripped again and stepped into her shower. The hot water stung as *cleansing* it streamed over her. She soaped and rinsed twice before she realized she was falling behind schedule. Luisa toweled off, trying to remove the exhaustion she felt. She resisted the impulse to collapse in her own bed; instead she hurried back down to the street. She picked up her coffee at the corner grocery where the owner's wife said good morning in Korean as she handed Luisa her fresh carnation. Luisa hopped on the downtown bus and from the window watched the sidewalk. It was alive with workers setting a rhythm that gathered energy as more people entered the flow. She arrived at work Wednesday morning, on time as usual.

Luisa pinned the white floor manager's carnation to her lapel, then looked over the order book in the stockroom. The rising voices of customers outside on the floor and the perky monotony of Muzak brought an unaccountable smile to her face. The phone rang and the air conditioning was too cold on her skin. She picked up the receiver. "Sportswear on Four, may I help you?"

"Yes. Do you have the Jones of New York blazer in a peach color?" asked a narrow, nasal voice.

Luisa gripped the telephone in her hand. "Yes, we have it in stock. Tell me what size. I'll put it aside for you until the end of the day. Your name, please? Fine, of course. I'll have it for you in the stockroom. Just come to Four and ask for the white flower." ✦

DON'T EXPLAIN

[handwritten: ∧ song by Billie Holiday / Look up lyrics]

[handwritten: Two weeks after Billies death]

Letty deposited the hot platters on the table effortlessly. She slid one deep-fried chicken, a club steak with boiled potatoes, and a fried porgy plate down her arm as if removing beaded bracelets. Each one landed with a solid clink on the shiny Formica in its appropriate place. The last barely settled before Letty turned back to the kitchen to get Savannah and Skip their lemonade and extra biscuits. Then to put her feet up. Out of the corner of her eye she saw Tip come in the lounge. His huge shoulders, draped in sharkskin, narrowly cleared the doorframe.

Damn! He's early tonight! she thought, but kept going. Tip was known for his extravagance; that's how he'd gotten his nickname. He always sat at Letty's station because they were both from Virginia, although neither had been back in years.

Letty had come up to Boston in 1946 and been waiting tables in the 411 Lounge since '52. She liked the casual community formed around it. The pimps were not big thinkers but good for a laugh; the musicians who played the small clubs around Boston often ate at the 411, providing some glamour—and now and then a jam ses-

[handwritten: Letty]

sion. The "business" girls were usually generous and always willing to embroider a wild story. After Letty's mother died there'd been no family to go back to down in Burkeville.

Letty took her newspaper from the locker behind the kitchen and filled a tall glass with the tart grape juice punch for which the cook, Henrietta, was famous.

"I'm going on break, Henrietta. Delia's takin' my station."

She sat in the back booth nearest the kitchen, beside the large blackboard which displayed the menu. When Delia came out of the bathroom, Letty hissed to get her attention. The reddish-brown of Delia's face was shiny with a country freshness that always made Letty feel a little shy.

"What's up, Miss Letty?" Her voice was soft and saucy.

"Take my tables for twenty minutes. Tip just came in."

The girl's already bright smile widened as she started to thank Letty.

"Go 'head, go 'head. He don't like to wait. You can thank me if he don't run you back and forth fifty times."

Delia hurried away as Letty sank into the coolness of the over-stuffed booth and removed her shoes. After a few sips of her punch she rested her head on the back of the seat with her eyes closed. The sounds around her were as familiar as her own breathing: squeaking Red Cross shoes as Delia and Vinnie passed, the click of high heels around the bar, the clatter of dishes in the kitchen, and ice cascading into glasses. The din of conversation rose, leveled, and rose again over the jukebox. Letty had not played her record in days, but the words spun around in her head as if they were on a turntable:

> Right or wrong don't matter
> When you're with me sweet
> Hush now, don't explain
> You're my joy and pain.

Letty sipped her cool drink; sweat ran down her spine, soaking into the nylon uniform. July weather promised to give no breaks, and fans were working overtime like everybody else.

She saw Delia cross to Tip's table again. In spite of the dyed red hair, no matter how you looked at her, Delia was still a country girl.

Delia

Long, self-conscious, shy—she was bold only because she didn't know any better. She'd moved up from Anniston with her cousin a year before and landed the job at the 411 immediately. She was full of fun, but that didn't get in the way of her working hard. Sometimes she and Letty shared a cab going uptown after work, when Delia's cousin didn't pick them up in her green Pontiac.

Letty caught Tip eyeing Delia as she strode on tight-muscled legs back to the kitchen. That lounge lizard! Letty thought to herself. Letty had trained Delia how to balance plates, how to make tips, and how to keep the customer's hands on the table. She was certain Delia would have no problem putting Tip in his place. In the year she'd been working at the 411, Delia hadn't gone out with any of the bar flies, though plenty had asked. Letty figured that Delia and her cousin must run with a different crowd. They talked to each other sporadically in the kitchen or during their break, but Letty never felt that wire across her chest like Delia was going to ask her something she couldn't answer.

She closed her eyes again for the few remaining minutes. The song was back in her head, and Letty had to squeeze her lips together to keep from humming aloud. She pushed her thoughts onto something else. But when she did she always stumbled upon Maxine. Letty opened her eyes. When she'd quit working at Salmagundi's and come to the 411 she'd promised herself never to think about any woman like that again. She didn't know why missing Billie so much brought it all back to her.

She heard the bartender, Duke, shout a greeting from behind the bar to the owner as he walked in. Aristotle's glance skimmed his dimly lit domain before he made his way to his stool, the only one at the bar with a back. That was Letty's signal. No matter that it was her break: she knew white people didn't like to see their employees sitting down, especially with their shoes off. By the time he was settled near the door, Letty was up, her glass in hand, and on her way through the kitchen's noisy swinging door.

"You finished your break already?" Delia asked.

"Ari just come in."

"Uh oh, let me git this steak out there. Boy, he sure is nosy!"

"Who, Tip?"

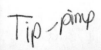
Tip - pimp

"Yeah. He ask me where I live, who I live with, where I come from, like he supposed to know me!"

"Well, just don't take nothing he say to heart and you'll be fine. And don't take no rides from him!"

"Yeah. He asked if he could take me home after I get off. I told him me and you had something to do." Letty was silent as she sliced the fresh bread and stacked it on plates for the next orders.

"My cousin's coming by, so it ain't a lie, really. She can ride us."

"Yeah," Letty said as Delia giggled and turned away with her platter.

Vinnie burst through the door like she always did, breathless and bossy. "Ari up there, girl! You better get back on station."

Letty drained her glass with deliberation, wiped her hands on her thickly starched white apron, and walked casually past Vinnie as if she'd never spoken. She heard Henrietta's soft chuckle float behind her. She went over to Tip, who was digging into the steak like his life depended on devouring it before the plate got dirty.

"Everything all right tonight?" Letty asked, her ample brown body towering over the table.

"Yeah, baby, it's all right. You ain't working this side no more?"

"I was on break. My feet can't wait for your stomach, you know."

Tip laughed. "*Break*. What you need a break for, big and healthy as you is!"

"We all get old, Tip. But the feet get old first, let me tell you that!"

"Not in my business, baby. Why you don't come on and work for me and you ain't got to worry 'bout your feet."

Letty sucked her teeth loudly, the exaggeration a part of the game they'd played over the years. "Man, I'm too old for that mess!"

"You ain't too old for me."

"Ain't nobody too old for *you*. Or too young, neither, looks like."

"Where you and that gal goin' tonight?"

"To a funeral," Letty responded dryly.

"Aw, woman, get on away from my food!" The gold cap on his front tooth gleamed from behind his greasy lips when he laughed. Letty was pleased. Besides giving away money, Tip liked to hurt people. It was better when he laughed.

The kitchen closed at 11:00. Delia and Letty slipped off their uniforms in the tiny bathroom and were on their way out the door by 11:15. Delia looked even younger in her knife-pleated skirt and white cotton blouse. Letty felt old in her slacks and long-sleeved shirt as she stood on Columbus Avenue in front of the neon 411 sign. The movement of car headlights played across her face, which was set in exhaustion. The dark green car pulled up and they got in quietly, both anticipating Sunday, the last night of their work week.

Delia's cousin was a stocky woman who looked about thirty-five, Letty's age. She never spoke much. Not that she wasn't friendly. She always greeted Letty with a smile and laughed at Delia's stories about the customers. Just close to the chest like me, that's all, Letty often thought. As they pulled up to the corner of Cunard Street, Letty opened the rear door. Delia turned to her and said, "I'm sorry you don't play your record on break no more, Miss Letty. I know you don't want to, but I'm sorry just the same."

Delia's cousin looked back at them with a puzzled expression but said nothing. Letty said goodnight, shut the car door, and turned to climb the short flight of stairs to her apartment. Cunard Street was quiet outside her window, and for once the guy upstairs wasn't blasting his record player. After her bath, Letty lay awake and restless in her bed. The electric fan was pointed at the ceiling, bouncing warm air over her, rustling her sheer nightgown.

Inevitably the strains of Billie Holiday's songs brushed against her, much like the breeze that moved around her. She felt silly when she thought about it, but the melody gripped her like a solid presence. It was more than the music. Billie was her hero. Letty saw Billie as big, like herself, with big hungers and a hard secret she couldn't tell anyone. Two weeks before, when Letty had heard that Lady was dead, sorrow had enveloped her. A door had closed that she could not consciously identify to herself or to anyone. It embarrassed her to think about. Like it did when she remembered how she'd felt about Maxine.

Letty had met Billie soon after she started working at the 411 when the singer had stopped in the club with several musicians on their way back from the Jazz Festival. There the audience, curious to see what a real, live junkie looked like, had sat back waiting for Billie to fall on her face. Instead she'd killed them dead with her liquid voice and rough urgency. Still, in the bar, the young, thin horn player had continued to reassure her: "Billie, you were the show, the whole show!"

Soon the cloud of insecurity receded from her face and it lit up with a center-stage smile. Once convinced, Billie became the show again, loud and commanding. She demanded her food be served up front, at the bar, and sent Henrietta, who insisted on waiting on her personally, back to the kitchen fifteen times. Billie laughed at jokes that Letty could barely hear as she bustled back and forth between the abandoned kitchen and her own tables. The sound of that laugh from the bar penetrated her bones. She'd watched and listened, certain she saw something no one else did. Vulnerability was held at bay, and behind that, a hunger even bigger than the one for food or heroin. Letty found reasons to walk up to the front—to use the telephone, to order a drink she paid for and left in the kitchen—just to catch the scent of her, the scent of sweat and silk emanating from her.

"Hey, baby," Billie said when Letty reached past her to pick up her drink from Duke.

"Henny sure can cook, can't she," Letty responded, hoping to see into Billie's eyes.

"Cook? She in these pots, sister!" the horn player shouted from down the bar, sitting behind his own heaping plateful of food.

Billie laughed, holding a big white napkin in front of her mouth, her eyes watering. Letty enjoyed the sound even though she still sensed something deeper, unreachable.

When Billie finished eating and gathered her entourage to get back on the road, she left a tip, not just for Henrietta but for each of the waitresses and the bartender. Generous just like the "business" girls, Letty was happy to note. She still had the two one-dollar bills in an envelope at the back of her lingerie drawer.

After that, Letty felt even closer to Billie. She played one of the few Lady Day records on the jukebox every night during her break. Everyone at the 411 had learned not to bother her when her song came on. Letty realized, as she lay waiting for sleep, that she'd always felt if she had been able to say or do something that night to make friends with Billie, it might all have been different. The faces of Billie, her former lover Maxine, and Delia blended in her mind in

hunger for something deeper (like Luisa's hunger for Naomi?)

holds on to tip Billie left her

regrets of not getting closer to Billie

Obsessions

half-sleep. Letty slid her hand along the soft nylon of her gown to rest it between her full thighs. She pressed firmly, as if holding desire inside herself. Letty could have loved her enough to make it better.

Sunday nights at the 411 were generally quiet. Even the pimps and prostitutes used it as a day of rest. Letty came in early to have a drink at the bar and talk with Duke before going to the back to change into her uniform. She saw Delia through the window as the younger woman stepped out of the green Pontiac, looking as if she'd just come from Concord Baptist Church. "Satin Doll" played on the jukebox, wrapping the bar in mellow nostalgia for the Sunday dinners they'd serve.

Aristotle let Henrietta close the kitchen early on Sunday, and Letty looked forward to getting done by 9:30 or 10:00 and maybe enjoying some of the evening. When her break time came, she started for the jukebox automatically. She hadn't played anything by Billie in two weeks. Now, looking down at the inviting glare, she knew she still couldn't do it. She punched the buttons that would bring up Jackie Wilson's "Lonely Teardrops" and went to the back booth.

She'd almost dropped off to sleep when she heard Delia whisper her name. Letty opened her eyes and looked up into the girl's smiling face. Her head was haloed in tight, shiny curls.

"Miss Letty, won't you come home with me tonight?"

"What?"

"I'm sorry to bother you, but your break time almost up. I wanted to ask if you'd come over to the house tonight...after work. My cousin'll bring you back home after."

Letty didn't speak. Her puzzled look prompted Delia to start again.

"Sometime on Sunday my cousin's friends from work come over to play cards, listen to music, you know. Nothin' special, just some of the girls from the office building down on Winter Street where she work, cleaning. She, I mean we, thought you might want to come over tonight. Have a drink, play some cards—"

"I don't play cards much."

"Well, not everybody play cards...just talk...sitting around talking. My cousin said you might like to for a change."

Letty wasn't sure she liked the last part—*for a change*—as if they had to entertain an old aunt.

"I really want you to come, Letty. They always her friends, but none of them is my own friends. They all right, I don't mean nothin' against them, but it would be fun to have my own personal friend there, you know?"

Delia was a good girl. Perfect words to describe her, Letty thought, smiling. "Sure, honey. I'd just as soon spend my time with you as lose my money with some fools."

By ten o'clock the kitchen was clean. Once they'd changed out of their uniforms and were out on the street Delia apologized that they had to take a cab uptown. She explained that her cousin and her friends didn't work on Sunday so they were already at home. Letty almost declined, tempted to go home. But she didn't. She stepped into the street and waved down a Red and White cab with brisk, urban efficiency. All the way uptown Delia explained that the evening wasn't a big deal and cautioned Letty not to expect much. "Just a few friends, hanging around, drinking and talking." She was jumpy, and Letty tried to put her at ease. She had not expected her visit would make Delia so anxious.

The apartment was located halfway up Blue Hill Avenue in an area where a few blacks had recently been permitted to rent. They entered a long, carpeted hallway and heard the sounds of laughter and music ringing from the rooms at the far end.

Inside, with the door closed, Delia shed her nervousness. This was clearly her home turf, and Letty couldn't believe she ever really needed an ally to back her up. Delia stepped out of her shoes at the door and walked to the back with her same long-legged gait. They passed a closed door, which Letty assumed to be one of the bedrooms, then came to a kitchen ablaze with light. Food and bottles were strewn across the blue-flecked table top. A counter opened from the kitchen into the dining room, which was the center of activity. Around a large mahogany table sat five women in smoke-filled concentration, playing poker.

Delia's cousin looked up from her cards with the same slight smile she displayed when she picked them up at work. Here it seemed welcoming, not guarded as it did in those brief moments in her car. She wore brown slacks and a matching sweater. The pink, starched points of her shirt collar peeked out at the neck.

Delia crossed to her and kissed her cheek lightly. Letty looked around the table to see if she recognized anyone. The women all seemed familiar in the way that city neighbors can, but Letty was sure she hadn't met any of them before. Delia introduced them, and each acknowledged Letty without diverting her attention from her cards: Karen, a short, round woman with West Indian bangles almost up to her elbow; Betty, who stared intently at her cards through thick eyeglasses encased in blue cat's-eye frames; Irene, a big, dark woman with long black hair and a gold tooth in front. Beside her sat Myrtle, who was wearing army fatigues and a gold Masonic ring on her pinkie finger. She said hello in the softest voice Letty had ever heard. Hovering over her was Clara, a large redbone woman whose hair was bound tightly in a bun at the nape of her neck. She spoke with a delectable Southern accent that drawled her "How're you doin'" into a full paragraph draped around an inquisitive smile.

Letty felt Delia tense again. Then she pulled Letty by the arm toward the French doors behind the players. There was a small den with a desk, some books, and a television set. Through the second set of glass doors was a living room. At the record player was an extremely tall, brown-skinned woman. She bent over the wooden cabinet searching for the next selection, oblivious to the rest of the gathering. Two women sat on the divan in deep conversation punctuated with constrained laughter.

"Maryalice, Sheila, Dolores...this is Letty. She work with me at the 411."

They looked up at her quickly, smiled, then went back to their preoccupations. Two of them resumed their whispered conversation; the other returned to the record collection. Delia directed Letty back toward the foyer and the kitchen.

"Come on, let me get you a drink. You know, I don't even know what you drink!"

"Delia?" Her cousin's voice reached them over the counter, just as they stepped into the kitchen. "Bring a couple of beers back when you come, okay?"

"Sure, babe." Delia went to the refrigerator and pulled out two bottles. "Let me just take these in. I'll be right back."

& Delia's cousin knew she was one too

"Go 'head, I can take care of myself in this department, girl." Letty surveyed the array of bottles on the table. Delia went to the dining room and Letty mixed a Scotch and soda. She poured slowly as the reality settled on her. These women were friends, perhaps lovers, like she and Maxine had been. The name she'd heard for women like these burst inside her head: *bulldagger.* Letty flinched, angry she had let it in, angry that it frightened her. "Ptuh!" She blew through her teeth as if spitting the word back at the air.

She did know these women, Letty thought, as she stood at the counter looking out at the poker game. They were oblivious to her, except for Terry. Letty finally remembered that that was Delia's cousin's name.

As Letty took her first sip, Terry called over to her, "We gonna be finished with this hand in a minute, Letty, then we can talk." This time her face was filled by a large grin.

"Take your time," Letty said. She went out through the foyer door and around to the living room. She walked slowly on the carpet and adjusted her eyes to the light, which was a bit softer. The tall woman, Maryalice, had just put a record on the turntable and sat down on a love seat across from the other two women. Letty stood in the doorway a moment before the tune began:

> *Hush now, don't explain*
> *Just say you'll return*
> *I'm glad you're back*
> *Don't explain...*

Letty was stunned. She realized the song sounded different among these women: Billie sang just to them. Letty watched Maryalice sitting with her long legs stretched out tensely in front of her. She was wrapped in her own thoughts, her eyes closed. She appeared curiously disconnected after what had clearly been a long search for this record. Letty watched her face as she swallowed several times. Then Letty sat beside her. They listened to the music while the other two women spoke in low voices.

Maryalice didn't move when the song was over.

"I met her once," Letty said.

"I beg your pardon?"

Maryalice → connection w/ Billie too

sexually charged → pathos

"Kinda met her. At the 411 Lounge where me and Delia work."

"Naw!" Maryalice said as she sat up.

"She was just coming back from a gig."

"Honestly?" Maryalice's voice caught with excitement.

"She just had dinner—smothered chicken, potato salad, green beans, side of stewed tomatoes, and an extra side of cornbread."

"Big eater."

"Child, everybody is when Henrietta's cooking. Billie was...," Letty searched for the words, "she was sort of stubborn."

Maryalice laughed. "You know, that's kinda how I pictured her."

"I figure she had to be stubborn to keep going," Letty said. "And not stingy, either!"

"Yeah," Maryalice said, enjoying the confirmation of her image of Billie.

Letty rose from the sofa and went to the record player. Delia stood tentatively watching from the doorway of the living room. Letty picked up the arm of the phonograph and replaced it at the beginning of the record. Letty noticed the drops of moisture on Maryalice's lashes, but she relaxed as Letty settled onto the seat beside her. They listened to Billie together, for the first time.   ✦

New Meaning
when w/ lovers?

Why
not
Terry

GRACE A.

great grandma
black & indian

S it down here, now." Grace pointed at the space on the carpet between her feet. The child hesitated for a moment, then sank onto the floor, her head barely reaching Grace's knees.

"Wait. Get up on this." The girl hopped up before the sentence was finished. Grace grabbed the narrow pillow she regularly used to rest her arm when she crocheted and dropped it to the floor. When the girl sat again she was not as low as before, but still her nose reached only the edge of the windowsill and the thick drapes hanging across the front of the flat.

Outside, the traffic—trolley cars and sedans—rumbled by on one of Boston's main thoroughfares. Tremont Street looped down almost from Egleston Square at the edge of Roxbury through housing projects, tenements, churches, triple-deckers, and shops owned and patronized by working-class colored families. It slid past Grace's front door in the South End toward the scandalous night life near Massachusetts Avenue, the even more torrid Combat Zone, and on into Chinatown. It circled the historic Boston Common and finally nestled in Boston's bustling downtown shopping district.

Grace's three-story, cold water, walk-up flat was large and bright, and located at just about the midway point on the trolley car line. The landlord didn't keep it up as well as he did other properties in more fashionable parts of town, but he couldn't neglect it completely, either. It was right next to a fire station, and the one black fireman stationed there had once told Grace to let him know if she was ever having trouble getting repairs. He'd make sure the city found out.

Black Housing

Grace had never taken him up on his offer. She swept the long flight of steps that led up to her flat, changed the light bulbs in the hall whenever it was needed, and hired a man to wash her windows every spring. She never liked owing anyone.

Listening to the news on the radio, Grace picked at the four braids that seemed eager to come loose. She sometimes wondered who all the white men were who talked on the radio: disc jockeys, newscasters, man-on-the-street-interviewers. There seemed to be a never-ending supply of modulated voices telling her what was going on in the world. She only half-believed what she heard but listened intently nonetheless, unwilling to miss some truth that might emerge. To Grace, the radio was more trustworthy than the television. She'd heard all the presidents on the radio.

She shifted in her seat to ease the stiffness in her right hip, and settled the girl in.

What the hell would she do with this round, silent eight-year-old? Her great-granddaughter. How could she be someone's great-grandmother? The thought made her chest ache. She'd just turned sixty, but she did not feel like an old woman. So who was she?

Grace pulled the brush around the edges of the soft, nappy hair. Umph, takes after her father's side. Never could stand combing this cotton, Grace thought impatiently. Her own long, gray hair was dyed black, close to its original. Her broad, nut-brown face was complemented by the thick, improbably dark hair as it nestled lightly on her forehead and at the back of her neck in a net. She'd always been a little embarrassed because it was not quite straight enough. That luck had fallen to her daughter and her granddaughter, the weight and texture of their hair inherited from the Ioway tribes and the Wampanoag of Cape Cod.

Hair

The girl tried to hold her neck stiff each time Grace hit a snag.

Her shoulders crept up around her ears as if she could hide inside herself.

"Let me do this." Grace pushed at the child's shoulders. They dropped so obediently it was disturbing.

"This isn't going to hurt."

Silence.

Grace continued brushing, feeling for knots and tangles more carefully. She was out of practice. When she'd agreed to take the child in she hadn't thought about this. Even if she had, what else could she have done? The child had been living with her father's mother; her own mother had gone off. Not gone off, Grace corrected herself; just living with someone else.

What could Grace do—Duke's mother had passed so quickly, and who else could take her? She hadn't thought about combing a child's hair in forty years. Hair. Clothes. Schoolwork. All of it loomed over Grace like a shifting cloud, not quite ominous, but dense, dimming everything. The girl's shoulders were up again.

"I'm not hurting you. Straighten out," Grace said in the clipped Bostonian accent that had reined in her Iowa drawl decades before.

Again obedience. Silence. *Suggesting abuse?*

What the hell am I supposed to say to her? Grace hadn't considered that either. She enjoyed her solitude after all the years alone. Her daughter, Lydia, wrote from New York regularly, but letters were something you could take in on your own time; their voices didn't intrude. She had two half-sisters in Boston, one not twenty minutes away, but they both talked so much—and about things they were ignorant of—that they rubbed Grace's nerves. Her time and her thoughts were always her own.

Except at the factory, of course. And they weren't interested in conversation there. It was good the child was old enough for school and that Tina Byars, around the corner, had agreed to keep her with her own grandchildren until Grace got home from work. Tina was the only white woman who lived in the neighborhood, but after thirty years of marriage to George, a black railroad worker, Grace hardly counted her as white anymore. All Tina Byars' grandchildren had sandy brown, fluffy curls.

She pulled the comb through the child's crinkly hair, surprised at how smoothly it went. Parted straight down the middle, then across the crown, it was like a little map. She pinned each section independently, to hold them in place while she braided one at a time. She'd discovered that on the first day. The child's hair was wild. Maybe not wild, but wiley. It crept out of its braids in a second if they weren't pinned down. It slipped out to stand all over her head if Grace didn't braid and pin them tightly.

It was an odd feeling—the child leaning stiffly against her knees as if she'd been plunked down from out of nowhere. And wasn't she? Grace looked down at the reddish brown frizz, puzzled to find herself in charge. Duke's mother died and here she was. She saw a large drop fall onto the child's brown arm. Her skin was a shade lighter than her father's, coppery like Grace's side of the family. *But his damn hair.*

"Are you crying?"

"Uh-uh."

"Don't say uh-uh. Say yes or say no."

"No." The voice was wavey with tears, but Grace did not dispute her. She didn't know what to say. The child had said 'no,' so that was that.

Grace tuned back into the radio news. Something about the White House and Little Rock. Grace only caught the end of it but knew that whatever it was, it was sure to make her angry. White men did such foolishness. She couldn't see how they'd ever got to run the country. Then they were on to McCarthy; more white people acting foolish.

"Eisenhower plays golf as much as he plays president," she said aloud without thinking. She was accustomed to being alone with her words.

The child giggled, and her body relaxed just a little.

"Turn this way."

The child wiped at her eyes quickly as she shifted on the pillow, turning away from the window to face the living room. Grace looked around her, trying to see the place as the child might. The air pulsed above the black metal space heater sitting in the center of the room. Behind it was the chair Grace had purchased from the secondhand store across the street just for the little girl. It was an overstuffed armchair covered in a textured blue fabric, with a small hassock. She'd set an old but ornate brass lamp beside it to create a place for the girl to do her homework.

On the mantelpiece facing the chair she'd sat a picture of her own daughter, Lydia, with the child's parents, so she'd know she wasn't just dumped off and forgotten. There might not be a lot of them, but they were loyal.

Grace felt the girl move back between her knees, this time almost snuggling, as if she were settling in, not afraid.

"Be still." The little body went rigid as the child looked back down at the pattern of the worn Oriental carpet.

Be still. Grace repeated it to herself, wondering why it sounded so familiar. She realized then it wasn't the words themselves, but the tone. Her own mother had sounded that way—tight, impatient. Her daughters were to be molded to her time, her needs. She had been able to convey that even on paper. It echoed in a small bundle of letters, lurking in the back of a drawer in Grace's secretary. Her mother had sent a note almost every day when Grace had fallen sick with influenza after her marriage.

For a month, each letter arrived, as formal as the one before. The letters, with their soft linen folds and light scent, were in some ways more personal than the occasional visits. The neat curl of the words shouted at Grace to trust in God and get well. Return to her duties as a wife.

Wife, Grace laughed to herself. She'd been fourteen years old, barely recovering from one of many fevers, when her mother had packed her few things, including the buckskin dress with little bright beads, and married her to the old man. John. He was Wampanoag, with little to his name except being great-nephew to the sachem Massasoit for whom the state was named.

John's primary appeal to Grace's mother was that tribal connection and his willingness to work, all of which she had taken more to heart than her daughter's feelings in the matter.

She only married me off to him so he could bury me. Grace was uncertain where to put her feelings about her mother's practical nature. Her mother had been relieved to find a Wampanoag with strains of black blood willing to marry another mixed-blood like himself.

Married at 14 to Wampanoag

Her notes read less like good wishes than they did an attempt to insure her investment.

Grace kept the letters to remind herself of how long ago it all was. It had always been easier for Grace not to answer, to pretend she couldn't think of anything to say to her mother about God or marriage, and hope her silence was taken as agreement. She knew her assessment of matrimony and church were easier kept to herself.

It wasn't such a bad bargain, Grace acknowledged. John was handsome enough. She still saw them in the mirror, standing side by side the day they were married. He was about six inches taller than she was, with a straight bearing, beautifully smooth skin, and shiny hair he kept cut short. He proved to be well-mannered and almost completely silent. He'd take his packet of bread and meat with him to work with barely a word and return in the night, exhausted and with even less conversation in him. Only rare occasions drew him out: the day he'd received a driver's license he'd been proud and almost loquacious. After borrowing their neighbor's car, John had donned a top hat and driven Grace around Cambridge, pointing out sites as if she'd just arrived from Iowa.

More often, Grace found John less forthcoming, and she had learned to hold her words back so he wouldn't be buried in the wave of her questions. Cambridge was so different from Iowa, and his New England coastal people were so unlike what she could remember of her own Plains people. Grace felt swollen with a curiosity she only revealed at opportune moments.

Two beautiful children had come from the union, if you counted the firstborn, a boy who drowned young. She never called his name, or even spoke it in her head anymore, but she remembered his glittering black eyes which were just like his father's. She could still recall how thin and light he'd felt as she held his body in her arms when they'd pulled him from the water-filled quarry. She'd buried him; then a few years later, John.

Their daughter, Lydia, who had their same flashing eyes, was who Grace counted on. She was like Grace's younger, secret self—her life was never held in check, she laughed out loud and ran around the country for any or no reason.

The girl was still beneath Grace's hand. It's not natural for a child to be so quiet, Grace thought. She couldn't remember Lydia ever being this guarded.

"We're about done," Grace said, resting her hand on the child's shoulder gently. She smiled at the plump skin, remembering what a child felt like. Then it frightened her, the softness, the dependence. Her stomach tightened. The dependence reminded her of the child's mother, Dolores. Something about dependence seemed to turn into domination for Grace. She finished the braid and pinned it down firmly. The girl continued sitting, her hands underneath her, staring at the carpet.

Grace rested her hand on the child's shoulder again. "There, that wasn't so bad, was it?"

"No."

"Let's see."

The girl stood, her eyes large and round. She turned to face her great-grandmother, her gaze full of curiosity and some fear. Grace was surprised at how much her eyes said even when the girl was quiet. *eyes*

"Did I tell you about my buckskin dress? The one my mother thought I'd get buried in?"

"Uh...I mean no."

"Tomorrow. When we do your hair."

"You had a real buckskin dress?" The child's eyes sparkled even as she still stood at attention.

"All young girls had them. They never thought I'd get old enough to outgrow it!" Gracias Archelina Sportsman Morandus, widow for forty years, chuckled softly. *Dedication*

The little girl smiled, beaming at the big square face gazing back at her. It no longer was a puzzle. Grace's eyes and mouth resolved themselves into something familiar, less frightening, less frightened.

Grace remembered that she had many stories to tell, at least as many as the books stacked haphazardly beside her sofa.

"Yeah, they never thought I'd last!" Laughter cracked from Grace like corn popping in a pan. "I'll tell you about that tomorrow." ✦

STEPS

War zone of black neighborhood

Ramona Edwards climbed the creaking stairs in the dim hallway, feeling much older than her thirty-five years. Her mother's flat, once her own home, waited for her on the third floor of the rundown Roxbury apartment building. So did Earl, her mother's husband.

At the second floor, Ramona stopped, peering around as if her childhood might unfurl from the pressed tin ceiling. Through the landing's empty window frame, the street she'd once loved was disordered, almost abandoned. What had been a busy black neighborhood now looked like a war zone from the late-night news. The black middle class had moved steadily away from the heart of Roxbury, leaving everyone else to fight city hall by themselves. They'd lost.

The door of 2B was thick with silence, unlike when the Cookes had lived there with their six brown, stair-step boys spilling out into the hallway to play, always calling Ramona downstairs although they knew she wasn't allowed to come back out after 8:00 P.M. Ramona ran her hand across the underside of the wooden banister. Even with her leather gloves on she could feel her nickname—Ray—where James Cooke had carved it one night when he was twelve, to prove he loved her. But he was just a boy, and Ramona had been fourteen. Her stepfather didn't allow her to play with boys.

Ramona's stomach roiled as her hand gripped the railing. Her fingers dug into the soft ridges of her name until she felt her hand cramp. She turned to look behind her: the stairs sagged steeply down toward the outside door, which stood open, its lock destroyed after many assaults. Empty crack vials swirled around on the tiny hallway's floor like a pestilence of leaves—dry, brittle litter. Ramona remembered her mother always calling out to her to shut the door.

"Keep the air and the trash outside, keep your butt inside," Betty Edwards Sherman used to shout down the stairwell when Ramona came in from the street, or when she went out, leaving Ramona peering at her through the railing from the third floor. Her mother had always sounded so protective.

Ramona turned back to the dark landing, walking on worn wood so familiar she could navigate the path in her sleep. 2A was also abandoned, its door padlocked. Hack marks marred the frame around the lock where someone had tried to get in. Mrs. Henderson had lived there when Ramona was thirteen.

She touched the ornate brass plate where the old doorknob had been. Although it was long gone, she could almost feel the cool curves of filigree on her fingertips. The same as the afternoon she'd stood outside Mrs. Henderson's door for an eternity, searching inside herself for the courage to knock. She'd held the knob, unable to turn it for so long it had gotten hot with the temperature of her small hand. She'd waited, hoping the words would come to her—a way to ask Mrs. Henderson about Earl.

Her mother, Betty, changed with Earl: she was awake, looking out at the world, not just at the old photo albums. Earl took Betty to Estelle's, where they listened to jazz combos, drank cocktails, and came home sweaty and laughing. Sometimes he took them both to the Strand movie theater at Roxbury Crossing, or downtown to the Paramount if there was something special. At first when Earl moved in with them, Ramona was happy. Her family finally looked like the ones in the books in school. It was fun, at ten years old, to finally have a father, not just a photograph and a military medal stuck in a drawer.

It was in the movies that it had started. A pat on Ramona's knee.

Then, sitting between them, he'd put one arm around her mother and the other around her, his hand resting on her small breast in the dark. Ramona sat still, thinking it was an accident, trying to watch the movie. The next time his fingers rubbed and pinched her breast and Ramona felt sick. She'd started to cry, but it was a long time before her mother noticed the tears. They only went home when Ramona said she didn't feel well.

From then on Ramona had structured her days and nights trying to avoid being alone with Earl. Once, she'd almost told her mother. They'd been shopping for groceries and stopped for a cold soda at the drugstore. As they'd sat in the dark wooden booth Ramona watched her mother thumb through a copy of the newest issue of *Sepia* magazine, then blurted out, "I don't like Earl."

Her mother had looked up, more puzzled than angry, as she answered, "He ain't here for your likes and dislikes, little lady. He's here for mine."

"He don't act right."

"Don't you pay any attention in school? 'He *don't*'? What kind of English is that?"

"He acts funny."

"What do you mean by 'funny'?"

Ramona looked away from her mother's piercing eyes. Over her shoulder she saw the streaked front window and read the letters backwards: ycamrahP llaH evorG. She loved the loopy scrawl when she passed by reading it from the street. Now the words felt alien; she knew what they meant but she couldn't say them.

"I know he's not your daddy, Ray. He can't act like him. He's just himself," Betty said, smiling at her memories of some night with Earl laughing beside her in the club with their friends. Or the scent of his Salem cigarettes wafting up on his breath as he slept beside her. Betty stared at her daughter as she complained about the man who'd brought her back to life. She was dark and thin like her dead father. With her ribbon untied, straightened hair sticking out from her head, she looked sweetly unruly, just as Ray had been.

Ramona saw her mother smiling inside and turned her attention back to her glass, sipping on her soda quietly.

Just jealous it's not us alone still, Betty thought, and picked up her magazine. Betty had never considered herself one of those women who had to have a man, but she knew she planned to keep this one.

Ramona had waited too long to speak that afternoon she stood outside the old woman's door. Mrs. Henderson, wearing her jacket and carrying her net shopping bag, opened the door abruptly just as Earl unlocked the outside door and started up the stairs.

"What is it, Little Ray?" Mrs. Henderson asked. She remembered Ramona's father, for whom the girl was named.

Ramona's mouth pulled open, but no words came out. Her small body was tight with her secret. Earl's footsteps on the second floor landing snapped the tension. Ramona said quietly, "Nothin', just wanted to say hi." Mrs. Henderson looked puzzled for a moment, then she glanced at Earl, who stopped short.

"Come in, child, and sit with me a while," Mrs. Henderson said, even though it was clear she was on her way out.

"She supposed to do her homework. You did your homework yet, Mona?"

Ramona was silent. She hated when he called her that.

"Come on, girl. We can't stand in this hall all afternoon. I got to get the cab back on the street."

Mrs. Henderson hesitated in the doorway, waiting for Ramona, who stood looking down at the floor.

Earl pushed her gently on the shoulder. "Betty gonna be home before you got your sums worked out, you better get a move on." He swept her in front of him, smiling at Mrs. Henderson as he went. Once upstairs, Ramona sat at the kitchen table immersing herself in her math worksheets as if they were a shield. Earl banged around making a sandwich. She'd known that as long as he was doing something, making noise, he wouldn't touch her.

She was enclosed so tightly inside herself, she'd barely heard the doorbell. Tossing his knife in the sink, Earl crossed impatiently to the living room. Ramona looked up when she heard Mrs. Henderson's voice asking Earl if she might borrow a measuring cup.

"I don't know where that kind of mess is."

"Ramona knows, she helps Betty."

"Here you go, Mrs. Henderson." Ramona yelled into the living room as she rummaged through the kitchen cabinet. Mrs. Henderson had a wide, flat smile as she took the old, battered tin measuring cup. Ramona wondered why she'd want it; she knew Mrs. Henderson possessed two perfectly good glass ones of her own because Ramona had helped her make cookies once.

"You makin' cookies, Mrs. Henderson?" Ramona asked, suddenly alert.

"I am, Little Ray, and since you have to stay and do your homework, I'm gonna check back up here and if you did good, I'll bring you some cookies. Deal?"

"Deal!" Ramona said, even though she never had to be pushed to do homework. She'd known the bargain was about something else.

From then on, Mrs. Henderson came upstairs in the afternoon whenever she could, often unannounced. Other times she'd call upstairs and ask Earl if Ramona could come down and help her do something. Soon Earl was coming home to eat his sandwich and then go right back out in his cab.

Ramona turned when she heard a noise behind her, but it was only the door downstairs banging in the wind. She pulled her shoulder bag in closer as if someone might come running in to grab it. She hadn't been back in this building since the day of her mother's funeral five years before.

Ramona had left home right after high school, worked her way west as far as Chicago, and maneuvered things so that she barely saw Earl. She'd purposefully lived in a studio apartment for ten years: there was only room for Betty to visit. She'd given her mother back the key to their flat and never shared a copy of the key to her own. When she came home to Boston she stayed in a hotel in the Back Bay and had lunch or dinner with Betty at restaurants. They'd sit and reminisce about the neighborhood, and not talk much about Earl.

They'd driven together to Mrs. Henderson's funeral. At the wake, Betty'd told everyone how good she'd been to them, how she'd made so many cookies for her and her daughter. Later, alone in the hotel, Ramona had cried wildly, burying her face in the pillow.

She'd not cried like that through most of the years living with her mother and Earl. Except once in the locker room at school. She couldn't remember now what had set her off, but she could feel the

[handwritten margin notes: Mrs. Henderson helps Ray out of abuse — mother too blind to notice]

Angela

heaving in her chest as she'd leaned into her locker, burying her sobs in her coat. Then she'd heard the sound of sneakers on linoleum. Coming down the row was Angela Gambino, who always hung out at the gym even though she didn't play basketball.

"What's shakin', girl? Why're you ballin' like that?" Her husky North End accent had sounded like a tugboat making its way toward her. Ramona had sobbed more violently, until Angela pulled her by the back of her sweater and sat her down on the bench.

"So give."

She'd shook her head as her shoulders quivered. "I can't," she'd said through snuffles. "I can't."

Angela had looked down at her for a minute, and Ramona thought she'd turn and leave. Black and white students didn't mix too much off the basketball court. When Ramona had looked up at her, Angela had stared back intently. The dark Italian curls around her face seemed electrified.

"Whatever it is, get out of it now, I'm tellin' you."

"You don't know—"

"Yeah, I do," Angela had said. "Just get the fuck out."

She'd said nothing else, walked to her locker, snatched her coat, and left. Angela stopped coming to school several weeks after that. Ramona heard that she'd run away and gone into the Army, but she hadn't known any of the kids from the North End well enough to ask.

Later, when she'd sat in class looking at the empty chair where Angela used to sit, Ramona had wondered what it would have been like if she'd told Angela everything. She could have told her how Earl still kissed her goodnight, rubbing under her flannel nightgown, pressing his anxious fingers first into her budding breasts, then into the baby fat of her thighs and the soft hairs which lead him to her opening. She lay rigid, her eyes squeezed shut but devoid of tears, as he touched her and himself, all the while talking in a low voice.

Could she and Angela have escaped together? Ramona laughed to herself, thinking no Italian from the North End was gonna be running off to save a black chick from Roxbury. But Angela knew, and still Ramona hadn't been able say it out loud.

No more than she could tell her mother when she'd been in the

→ Letty's thoughts w/ Billie

save each other

hospital. The hard curve of Betty's Boston accent had softened with age and illness. Ramona had been used to her mother talking loudly, her words filling up their rooms, but everything was quiet as Betty looked at her with questions. Occasionally she'd talk about how good Earl had been to them. Then she'd say, "I ain't forgetting your father, that's not what I mean. But Earl been good to us." She'd look at Ramona, waiting for agreement. Ramona said nothing. To speak would have been to scream. Betty had died in Boston City Hospital, holding Ramona's hand, thinking Earl was on his way, even though she'd never seen Ramona and Earl in the hospital room at the same time.

Ramona had returned to her hotel. She let Earl make all the arrangements, then right after the funeral flew back to Chicago to look for a larger apartment.

When Earl called five years later, Ramona had listened to his voice on the answering machine with no intention of calling back. After the third time, Earl left this message: "I don't know where you got yourself to, Mona, but if you want this stuff of your mother's, you better get back over here 'fore I toss it out."

Ramona turned from Mrs. Henderson's door and looked to the top of the stairs. They seemed shorter, less wide than when she was a girl. For a moment she was lonely for the old building, the neighbors who were all gone now, having ecaped the decay. But time had also fled; it was no longer Ramona's home. It was Earl's, and he was leaving too.

Ramona expected to hear her mother's voice, or the sound of the Cookes laughing together behind their door; instead there was only scattered noise from the street. Ramona climbed faster, knowing it would not be comfortable to still be here after dark. The old anxiety began to rise inside her as she neared the apartment's front door, pulling at her stomach and chest. What was worth subjecting herself to this feeling? She couldn't remember exactly what she might want from her mother's things. What might she expect to find? Maybe a dress? A cigarette lighter? High-heel pumps? The pictures that came to mind weren't of Betty but of Hollywood pinups from the '40s and '50s—Dorothy Dandridge or Joan Crawford. Ramona knew Betty had no furs or diamonds, and if she'd had, Ramona imagined Earl would have pawned them by now, or given them to another woman.

When Ramona looked in the mirror she knew she looked a lot like her mother—chestnut brown skin, thick hair—except hers was cut close in a natural. Her almond-shaped eyes were dark like Betty's, and her long thin arms and legs had developed sinewy muscle. She had the trim body of an athlete, or a carrier of books. Only recently had Ramona begun to see her smile enough to recognize it as Betty's, too. But she still couldn't remember what any of the individual items might be that were her mother's "things."

Ramona forced a sick feeling into the background so she could focus and spend as little time as possible inside. She felt ready to face Earl; he was nothing to her now. Her skin barely remembered what his touch felt like.

She knocked firmly on the door of 3A, like a stranger delivering a package. Waiting for Earl to answer, she looked back down the stairs as if Mrs. Henderson might pop her head out. Earl swung the heavy, old door back with a flourish, smiling broadly.

"So, the little girl returns home. And just in time." Earl stepped back and opened the door wider. A few boxes stood neatly stacked behind him in the living room. Ramona felt like a child again. As she stared past the living room couch, down the hall to the kitchen, she almost expected to see Little Ray sitting at the table doing homework. She forced herself to walk in.

"You want a drink? When'd you get in?"

"No. Did you pack up all her stuff already?"

"Naw, just mine. I'm taking some things over...over to my place this weekend."

Ramona looked at Earl as he stumbled on his words. "Does your new girlfriend have any children?"

He gave a satisfied laugh. "She likes to run around too—" He stopped, understanding what Ramona asked. "No," he continued, his voice tight, the laughter snatched back.

Ramona watched his light brown eyes as his gaze darted around the room, avoiding her. His slacks were sharply creased, topped by a knit sport shirt as usual. He still wore the simple gold band that Betty had given him on the ring finger of his left hand. Ramona remembered trying not to feel his hand on her breast in the movies. She remembered catching a glimpse of light flickering off the ring as she'd stared straight ahead at the screen.

"I'm down the Prudential now. I left that cab stuff. It was weird driving, knowing old Betty wasn't gonna come running down the stairs if I honked the horn. Hop in and drive with me half the night. We used to do that a lot—later, after you left, I mean." Earl talked, filling the air to keep the past from catching him.

"Where are her things?"

"Right where she left them. The closet, in the bureau. Figured you'd wanna go through."

Ramona walked down the short narrow hall. It was obvious that Earl was already spending a lot of time elsewhere. The bed was stripped, and all the clothing was gone except Betty's.

"I got a couple bags here, case you didn't bring nothing to carry stuff."

Ramona hadn't thought about that at all. She shoved her gloves into her purse and took the brown shopping bag from Earl's out-stretched hand.

"Making pretty steady money down the Prudential. Working se-curity. Did I tell you that?"

It was safe as long as he kept making noise, Ramona thought, sliding the hangers which held her mother's dresses across the rod. She breathed in the faint scent of Chanel wafting out of the closet. Tears pushed forward, but she held them back. None of the clothes were anything special, the frayed legacy of a woman who'd worked hard all her life. What she remembered wouldn't be in a wardrobe: the vision of her mother, studiedly casual, waiting for her on the sidewalk after school with a shopping cart full of brightly wrapped presents for her twelfth birthday. Or the laughing curl of Betty's voice after the infrequent visits from her dead husband's brother. Betty had invariably said as he'd hurry down the stairs, "Your daddy was a much better man, believe me."

The day Ramona left home Betty had held her tightly, quickly, and said, "You're a good girl, Little Ray. You always been a good girl." At the time, Ramona had wondered if her mother was thank-ing her for not making trouble about Earl. She'd thought over and over about the sound of Betty's voice, its inflections echoing in her head. She never could decide for sure. But the sound of her saying it rang ambivalently in her mind sometimes when she was alone.

Ramona shut the closet door.

"Goodwill, huh?"

"Whatever you want to do with them."

"Betty sure was a dresser. Can't really tell from the clothes just hanging there. But when she put on a dress, man it was put..."

Ramona ignored Earl's words and turned to the bureau. There was nothing on top, but inside the first drawer was her mother's cream-colored Bakelite hairbrush. Ramona dropped it into the shopping bag. Two wooden cigar boxes from Cuba sat snugly side by side. They held earrings and necklaces more brightly colored than anything Ramona ever wore. The library was a quiet place, and she was usually dressed to match, at work or not. She popped simple gold hoops into her ears every day. But here were large purple discs, red berries, and green polka-dotted plastic. The swirl of vibrant color made Ramona feel slightly faint. She gripped the edge of the bureau.

"I think she had some pearls in there somewhere. I didn't go looking, but I think she had some pearls."

Ramona drew in her breath, then continued sifting through the boxes. A short double strand of pearls, pink shining through luminescence, lay wrapped in facial tissue beside a loop of lime green pop beads. Ramona snapped the boxes closed and put them in the bag. She moved quickly through the next drawer, which was full of odds and ends, then knelt to open the bottom drawer. She felt Earl move closer behind her.

"I'll be done here in a minute," Ramona said, looking over her shoulder at his shadow on the floor.

"I'll make some coffee. You drinking coffee yet?" Earl said, laughing as if she'd just made drinking age.

Ramona didn't answer or look at Earl as he left the bedroom. It amazed her how much he had not changed: the same dapper clothes, a slight smell of scotch oozing from his pores, his bantering talk sliding over the surface of things. She'd thought he might be sagging, ruined, like the apartment building. When she was a child with her eyes closed he'd seemed to be a monster torturing her, but looking at him now he was simply casual, self-absorbed.

Folded neatly in the bottom drawer were a stack of scarves and handkerchiefs. When she saw them she remembered her mother always tucking one of the hankies in her purse after daubing it with Chanel. The scarves—chiffon and silk—were added to her outfits at the last minute. Betty would tie one around her neck, with no thought of matching its color to her blouse or dress. The arbitrariness of the selection completed her look. Her dresses weren't her dresses without the scarves. Ramona lifted the neat stacks and placed them on top of the cigar boxes. At the bottom of the drawer she saw a small velvet drawstring bag. She loosened the drawstring and slid out the medal: a tiny rifle on a blue backing and an oak leaf cluster. As a child the medal was too closely attached with her father's absence for Ramona to feel comfortable with it. Now the untarnished metal and soft blue held all that he and her mother had been to each other. She slid it down into the side of the bag.

When she walked into the kitchen Earl was pouring Johnny Walker into a glass, not making coffee. She moved around him to the cabinet above the sink. The dishes her mother had gotten piece by piece from the supermarket were still there. She looked through the next cabinet at the glasses. Not crystal, but not jelly glasses: sets of six, short and tall, tiny juice glasses with wedges of fruit painted on the side.

"So you got nothing to say." Earl spoke after swallowing his drink in a gulp.

Ramona thought of all the times she'd told him to stop and he'd laughed, all the times she'd struggled to find the words to tell her mother what he did, and all the time she'd spent recounting the stories to strangers who tried to help her shed the terrors he'd left behind.

"Not really," she said.

"'Spose I got something to say?"

"Then you better get it out while I'm here, 'cause I'm almost gone."

Ramona was pleased to hear no tremor in her voice although her chest felt so tight she wasn't sure how the air was getting in and out. She closed the cabinet and opened the drawer beside the sink. The tinny forks, knives, and spoons lay in neat rows, along with a couple of wooden utensils and a can opener.

"I got my new address and phone number here. I'm puttin' it in your bag. So you can know where I am."

Ramona said nothing as she continued looking through the drawers and cabinets.

"You always give me such a hard row to hoe, you know that? I couldn't never get on your good side. You didn't wanna talk to me. You know that? You..."

Ramona turned to look at him. Her eyes were slits of ice as she took him in. A small man, she thought. Maybe she'd known that even back then. Maybe that's why she'd survived. Ramona was surprised by her own tight chuckle.

"Do you know how many times I wished you were dead? Did you want me to tell you that?"

"Aw, Mona, come on."

"If you call me Mona again I'm going to hit you with this." She watched him gulp air this time and take a step back. She set down the cast-iron frying pan she'd just found.

"Ramona, okay. Relax." Earl kept smiling as he always did.

Still watching Earl, she felt between the sink and the refrigerator. There, where her mother had always kept them, were plastic bags; she slid the frying pan inside one. She reached into her brown shopping bag, took out the slip of paper with Earl's new address on it, tossed it onto the kitchen table, and set the pan on top of the scarves. The table was marbled gray with a pink stripe around the edge. Once, she had stared at that strip of pastel until it dissolved as she pretended to study.

She looked up at Earl. It was exhilarating not to feel like that kid anymore. Still, she had to struggle to control the shaking in her hands. She squatted by the cabinet beneath the sink.

"I'm just saying....," Earl poured himself another drink and sipped it this time, "...like you ain't never had to act so high and mighty, Miss Ramona." The liquor had twisted his charm into a snarl.

Ramona dug around the sink behind the cleansers and sponges. The old tin measuring cup, almost full of water, sat beneath the crook of the drain pipe. She stood holding it in her trembling hand.

"Had a little leak," said Earl, laughing. "Can't get nothing fixed now, that's for sure."

Ramona dumped the water into the sink and rinsed out the measuring cup. She poured dish soap in it then scrubbed until the battered aluminum was almost shiny. She dried it with a paper towel and wrapped it in another before slipping it into her purse. Earl watched, maybe remembering Mrs. Henderson, maybe not.

Ramona left the kitchen. Earl set his glass down and followed. She could feel him wanting to say something. She hoped he'd be quiet for a change. She glanced around, no longer recognizing the rooms. In the foyer she opened the door to the hallway and stepped out.

"So that's it? You just walkin'?"

"Earl, what you got to say to me?"

"I'm just trying to get you to say something to me. I helped raise you and you ain't got the courtesy..."

"Earl, this is what I have to say to you: I was ten years old when you came to live with us and put your hands on me. That's what I got to say to you."

He reached toward her shoulder.

"If you touch me I will scream this house down."

Earl stepped back, circled, and placed himself between Ramona and the steps, needing to make her stay. She set down the shopping bag, took her leather gloves out of her purse, and put them on as she waited for him to move.

"I...uh...you were always so sweet. I..." His voice was hoarse with scotch and other things. Ramona moved back and peered at him as if he were a tiny, squiggling thing. His eyes hardened. Earl reached out, grabbed her arm.

The desperation of his touch plunged Ramona into a scarlet wave of anger. She screamed. Piercing horror and fear bellowed from her throat. Years of it filled the empty hallway, rattling the few remaining panes of glass. She screamed with her eyes wide open as if she were singing. Tears slipped out of the corners, rolled down into her mouth, feeding her scream as it built. It became a seamless, rolling shriek that sucked in the air around it.

Earl stumbled away from her, drawing his hand to his ears. He slipped backward down the first step, a look of disbelief in his eyes. Ramona came to the end of her breath. She gasped for air as the scream drained away from her, echoing around them. Earl continued to fall. At first it looked as if he were trying to play a trick on her, make her laugh at a pratfall. But he tumbled over backward in a way no man of his years could do so easily. He slid the last few steps to the second-floor landing and lay face down on the scarred wood. Ramona watched for a moment, wondering if he'd get up, unable to tell if he was moving.

She switched her purse with the measuring cup to her left shoulder, holding onto the shopping bag with one hand and the banister with the other. She walked down the stairs toward Earl. The crackling of the paper bag as it brushed her pants when she walked made it impossible to hear if he was breathing or not. She stepped carefully over him, past Mrs. Henderson's door, on to the next flight of stairs. The sound of brown paper rustled in her ears, blocking out the dry, creaking wood and the wind outside. Ramona continued down to the first floor and out the door of her mother's old building for the last time. ✦   *Earl dead!*

OUNCE OF CHARM

O kay, deal the cards. Like I was saying...what you mean we all got to be at the table? Shiiit! All right, lemme finish the story. I can't believe y'all ain't heard this already. She musta told it a thousand times. Like I said, I shouldn'ta been surprised. I mean how many times can you count on scientists really knowing what they're doin'?

The way she tells it she was basically happy with how the world was turning. A regular nine to five at the Department of Human Services, which was a joke since any time a city employee acts human, or like she's helping another human obtain some services, the wall of bureaucracy falls on her like the old ton of bricks. But you know government really is about the only place a black woman gonna find a job in this town. Don't get me wrong, Juanita is good at the people thing. You know when you hear about folks goin' in and shootin' up city workers cause somebody wasn't acting right around their check or stamps, whatever? I personally seen Juanita short-circuit two or three of them massacres all by herself.

Anyhow, she does the church thing every once in a while just to check in with the ancestors, house party now and then, visits from relatives back in Texas. What's missing? Romance, of course.

Her friends kept telling her she was good lookin' and smart. They were as puzzled as she was about why she couldn't find a man. She got that round, brown look anybody would snatch up quick. But they shoulda known that when it comes to a woman searching for a man, smart cancels out good-lookin' like a sixteen-wheeler splats a possum.

Hey, Juanita is not a depressed kind of woman, you know that yourself. Opposite. When she meets the brambles, she makes a new path. That's her all over, always has been far as I can tell. Yo! Can't we deal the cards. Y'all disrupting my luck.

All right, all right. So it wasn't like she didn't meet men all the time. There's the middle management at work, the guys at church, the guys who volunteered at the food delivery project she works for a couple hours a week. Then there's...well, hell, it don't matter now.

It was kind of a joke at first. They had these ads all over the radio. You couldn't get away from them. Juanita listened and didn't listen. She wasn't the type who was what you call "on the make." But she found herself at a perfume counter at Target and there it was: Charm. Just like she heard on the radio. Really expensive—an ounce set her back as much as that leather bag you carrying. But there it sat. Charm.

How am I supposed to know? She went for it, that's all. She sure got enough goin' for her on her own. I knew that soon as she come to work in the building.

On the radio they kept saying it made you irresistible, you know, to the opposite sex. Some kind of gnomes. Pheronomes...something ...mixed in it. Like a smell you can't smell that you supposed to have anyway. And it 'sposed to trigger something in somebody else and they can't help themselves. A dash behind the ear and they after you. Yeah, I always been partial to musk myself.

Anyway, she tries it. Ounce of Charm, to go. Well, from what I can get out of her she dabs a speck of Charm on her neck and before she can finish putting on her pantyhose she felt her heart flutter. She checked the mirror, wondering if she was lookin' sick. But there she was—bronze amazon in the pink, so to speak. Her breasts were heavin', though. The swell of them in her bra just captured her attention. She smiled at herself, and next thing she finds she's sitting on the floor in front of the mirror.

She touched her nipples and they were hard, like little candies. Well, girl, she leaned back and opened her legs. Her thatch of curlies was already wet. First, she rubbed the lips, and then, when she touched the hard button, she knew she'd hit gold. Back and forth she went, like she did this every day. Those fingers found places she had not even thought about. Neighbors must have wondered what was goin' on up in her flat, 'cause she called in sick and spent the day exploring. Exploring her body, I mean. You gonna deal?

Hell, that wasn't the best of it. First she didn't think it was connected. To the Charm stuff. She thought maybe she was just hot, hormone shifting, who knows. But the next day when she goes to work, just to be sure, she waited 'til she was getting ready to come in the building.

You know the building. Looks like a fancy warehouse. I sit there all during my shift, in my security uniform, trying not to scare the folks to death. I hate wearing that thing. The pants never fit right and that badge, umph. Don't mean a damn thing, 'cept to people already too vexed as it is. So I see her come and go every day. This time I notice she stopped just before coming through the door. I wondered what she was doin'. Then she come on like she always does. Says to me, "Mornin', Idell," just like usual and goes on up in the elevator.

Well, let me cut to the chase. Right. It works, like a charm, so to speak. But of course who falls for her first? You got it. See, they kept saying it would make a person of the opposite sex fall for you. Hell, scientists don't even know what the opposite sex is!

Juanita, being Juanita, didn't even bat an eyelash at the invitation. Danced the night down to the nubs like she always been hanging out 'cross the bay with the girls at the SisterSpace. They thought disco was dead! Not Juanita. It was like she was possesed by Sylvester and the Weather Girls.

Then, after hours, she was still lively as a tiger on visiting day.

You ain't telling that story again?

Yeah, Juanita, I am.

Idell, why you don't let me tell my own story?

Well, go ahead. They waiting to deal.

So I go dancin.'

I already told that part.

Oh. Well, she asked me to come back to her flat and I said yes, 'cause I hadn't figured on BART being closed down at that hour. I couldn't even tell what I was saying yes to. But she was something. Turns out her people from Texas too. So there we went and she kissed me soon as the door was closed. I thought the top of my head was gonna fly off. We went into her room quiet, 'cause she had roommates.

I was a little nervous, so I kinda looked out the window. Child, there was this view! I mean I've seen a view, but there was something about the night and all the lights. Many years as I've lived here, how many times you think I looked out and thought, This is my city? Not many, I'm a tell you. It was like I was seein' a city I ain't never seen before.

But girlfriend wasn't into sightseeing. She was busy taking off all my clothes. I think that was what got me, too. Nobody ever did that before. I was laying on the bed, on top of a gold kind of comforter, and she start kissing me at the bottom, working her way up. I couldn't catch my breath. She was licking my knees and rubbing my thighs and I closed my eyes at first. Then I wanted to see what was going on. When her lips touched my breasts, child! And started all over again. She bit and nibbled on my breasts until I wasn't sure they were part of my body. I watched her get up then and take off her shirt and slacks. I realized I had never really looked at another woman's thing before.

Thing...you know. I was hypnotized. She was so dark down there, yeah, down there. Like a pool I could sink into and never return. But I didn't see too much of it right then 'cause she laid down again. On top of me. Something about the weight of her took my breath away. I don't mean she was heavy! Just made me want to stop breathing and pay attention. She kissed me on the mouth this time. Her lips were like sucking on a fruit pie.

My mind was completely taken up with them, so when she touched me I jumped. Her fingers smoothed the hairs inside my thigh, then around...you know. I was scared I was dripping onto the pretty gold comforter. Funny the things you think about, ain't it?

She didn't say a word, just plunged right on in, like she knew I was waiting. Her finger became two, then three, moving in and out. And my hips moved to meet her. I wrapped my arms around her back. I was digging the way her muscles rippled, and then her butt! Girl's cute, round mound. But mostly I just opened up to take her in.

I was ready to holler. She pushed deep inside, then out, touching the edges, pushing in again. I felt her hand swell inside me, filling me, taking me to the top. And I screamed. At least I started to. Her hand clamped down over my mouth like it was a stickup. Set it off!

Girl, she held her hand over my mouth and my eyes popped open. She said *ooh, baby* and kept moving inside me, hard and fast. One hand pinned me to the bed and the other worked like a Texas oil drill—slick, deep, and steady. Harder, harder she pounded, and my scream kept coming into her hand.

Damn, Juanita, you love to get graphic don't you?

You the one started telling it, Idell. Five years, and she still blushing over a bottle of perfume.

Come on now, just deal the cards.

How come you always get so shy when the story gets to the part with you in it?

The woman just asked me what I give you for our anniversary.

And what was you gonna say?

I was gonna say Juanita always had all the charm she needs, baby. That's why I always give you lilac water.

Okay, deal the cards.   ✦

WATER WITH THE WINE

is this representative of Gomez herself ↑

*A*lberta applied fresh red to her lips under the glare of the bathroom fluorescents and smoothed the soft folds of her tan linen skirt. She sighed, pushed one imaginary strand of hair behind her ear, then drew a deep breath, gathering her energy for the final event—a small reception for out-of-town speakers given by a local women's writing group. Although she'd been leery of being the only black writer and the only out lesbian on the program, Alberta was pleased with her presentation on sexuality in women's literature. But she could have predicted that: *SEX* put sex in the title and anything perks up.

She let herself relax for the few minutes it took to walk back down the corridor to the college's small reception room. Once there, she set herself for the barrage of light banter and personal questions that visiting writers always confronted. Tomorrow she'd board a plane for one more speaking engagement, then it would be home to Boston to collapse for a day before settling into grading the final papers of the semester.

Alberta reached across a table to refill her glass with white wine.

(margin note: who? white women?)

Her hand met the carafe at the same time as a young woman's. Alberta recognized her from the question-and-answer period during the presentation. She was short, with cropped dark hair and the body of a runner. Tonight she looked older, dressed in soft leather trousers and a silk shirt. But Alberta had not forgotten the brilliant smile and sharp eyes.

The young woman introduced herself as Emma and said, "I bet you'd give anything to sit down."

"How can you tell?"

Emma eased Alberta toward one of the couches against the wall, away from the swirl of writers and students.

(margin note: stories) "I really appreciated your frankness when you were asked about sadomasochism and lesbian feminism," Emma said.

Alberta laughed. It still startled her to have these terms blurted out by young students even when she herself had used them so casually in the lecture hall. At fifty, Alberta continued to surprise herself with the things she knew and said.

"Well," she started, "unlike some, I don't think there are topics that should not be discussed. We can't afford the luxury of Victorian attitudes. In fact, if it's difficult to discuss, all the more reason to bring it up."

Alberta's glance caught the silver labyris hanging against Emma's tanned skin at the neck of her shirt. "Living out here I'm sure you can understand that."

"Sure, in the abstract, or on a one-to-one basis, but being put on the spot like that...you were the only black writer and then the only one doing a presentation on sexuality. I don't know what I'd do. "

Alberta looked more directly at the woman, who was probably younger than twenty-five and had an impish smile.

"Somebody's always going to be asked to represent something. We might as well prepare ourselves." Weariness threaded through Alberta's attempt to sound like the earth mother everyone expected. The decades between the two of them felt like a chasm.

(margin note: what does she represent) "Maybe you just start to represent yourself, professor." Emma's smile had faded. She peered intensely at Alberta as if she understood all that it took to get on a plane and place herself in front of a university audience like a target.

Is this the most romance novel ever by written writers featured white charac drawn + black romance is a new trend

Alberta smiled politely. Emma continued looking at her, her expression unchanged. It was a gaze that poked and probed the silence between them. Alberta turned away, unable to make whatever declaration Emma's look was insisting upon and caught her ex-lover, Elizabeth, watching them from across the room. Although she'd been instrumental in having Alberta invited to the conference, she'd studiously avoided her.

By the time Alberta finished wondering about Elizabeth, Emma was back to the panel discussion, asking questions about Audre Lorde. She didn't use the hushed tones that nascent writers sink to but drove her inquiries as if she knew the writer's work intimately.

"But if, as you said, the impulse to dramatic sexual expression, as you called it, is present in all of us, why don't you see it more in young black writers? Why is it primarily prevalent in the writing of white women?"

"Socialization, sublimation, any number of reasons. Not seeing it explicitly in someone's writing or conversation doesn't mean it doesn't exist. Some people are more private than others, even within themselves."

Just then Alberta caught Elizabeth's glance and thought how true that was. Professor Elizabeth Bateson was so private even she didn't know her own feelings.

An old memory burst open inside Alberta, messy and troubling, *left behind* like a split garbage bag. She and Elizabeth at dinner: "I've got the Missouri job." Her lack of emphasis, the ease, said the rest—Alberta would be left behind.

That had been over a year ago, and Elizabeth still didn't acknowledge how hurt Alberta had been. This invitation implied there was no reason for anger. Alberta ignored the subtext and simply accepted the check, then added the college's name to her résumé. If Elizabeth wanted to avoid unpleasantness by substituting a formal professional relationship for honesty, I can bear a chill with the best of them, Alberta thought. "Fine," she said out loud.

"Great," Emma said, her smile returning.

"What?"

"I was asking if you'd like to go for coffee or something to wash out the taste of collegiate jug wine."

"Oh."

Conversation swirled around them and they had to lean a little closer to be heard. Alberta found herself trying not to gaze at the soft swell of Emma's breasts as they rose and fell with excitement beneath her red silk blouse. Alberta looked down at her watch. It was still early, but she'd done her duty here. Her plane wasn't until 1:00 the next afternoon. She nodded gratefully; they stood and moved toward the door. Elizabeth reached them just as Alberta turned back, remembering she should say good-bye to the department chair.

"Berta, just let me know when you're ready. I'll get you back to your hotel." Elizabeth's voice was ripe with calculation.

"No need, Liza," Alberta's smile blazed. Elizabeth hated being called by her nickname in front of colleagues.

"I've got a ride right here. This was a great event. You should be proud. I'll call you when I finally get back to Beantown."

She stood on her toes, planted a quick kiss on the silver hair at Elizabeth's temple, and darted toward Emma, who was already half-way down the hall. In five minutes they were seated in Emma's battered Chevrolet. Twenty minutes later she was surprised when they pulled up in front of a small, wood-frame house on a shaded street.

"We might as well have it here. I don't think anything's left open in this town at this hour. Except maybe the leather bars."

Alberta, anxious to leave behind the emotions Liza stirred in her, nodded with curiosity. They climbed old wooden stairs and entered the quiet darkness of the house.

"I thought my housemate might be home, but it looks like she's out."

"When I had housemates, 'out' was the best thing I could say about them."

"She's all right. Just a little young."

Alberta smiled to herself and said nothing. Once seated on the couch, she accepted a glass of iced fruit juice instead of coffee. Alberta asked about Emma's graduate work in American literature and listened as her enthusiasm bubbled over the hum of an old fan and a Joan Armatrading tape Emma had clicked on. Books lined the walls, and stacks of papers were strewn across a desk at the other end of the room, testifying to the research Emma talked about.

are blacks looking for new controversy to escape blackism

"I think you must need some theatrical training to do this kind of thing, going around to campuses answering personal questions. You just drew a breath and sounded like discussing nipple piercing was the most natural thing in the world."

"Believe me, it's not casual. I used to be so nervous my voice quavered. I see those faces out there trying to find a discretely academic way to put me down. But then I see the other faces. Like yours—more curious than afraid."

"A lot of them confuse discussing with advocating."

"Who needs to advocate? People find their own expressions of desire whatever the moral majority or academics condemn. If I wanted to stop whatever the majority disapproved of, I'd have to start by figuring out how not to be black."

"Don't you think that's where the comparisons between movements break down? I mean, I have figured out a way not to be poor. I can leave that behind. You can't not be black."

"You think you can leave things behind, Emma. You can't, really."

"As much as I'm paying for this degree, I better!"

They laughed again. As she relaxed, Alberta realized how tired she was and kicked off her shoes. Emma slid down to the carpet and began massaging her feet. Alberta didn't protest but rested her head on the back of the worn sofa and let her mind wander. Liza appeared briefly, but Alberta pushed her to the side as she'd done often during the past year.

"Ticklish?"

"No, just thinking."

"What?" Emma asked.

"Um...what Liza, Professor Harris, would say if she could see us now. I think this could be construed as an act of exploitation!"

"Or an act of seduction," Emma responded.

"Who's seducing whom?" Alberta kept her voice steady, enjoying the feel of Emma's hand on her calf.

Emma kneeled on the edge of the sofa, towering over Alberta's face. "I'll seduce first, then you can seduce next, just to keep it egalitarian." She leaned down and stopped any response with her mouth.

Alberta was startled, uncertain how she wanted to respond. She was used to come-ons from students. She had even been in tight *compare to Delaney— wow! difference*

Now back to sexuality

spots that required embarrassing but firm rejections. But she'd not been here before. She wanted the kiss and knew it as soon as she felt Emma's hand. Still she was torn between many things: Liza's horror, which lurked somewhere in the distance, and her own sense of propriety. A strict code of behavior had often helped her through tough emotional situations, but now it clung to her with the same discomfort as one of those panty girdles she'd given up so long ago.

With Emma's mouth pressed to hers, Alberta felt something she hadn't experienced since Liza'd left her—desire. Emma then pulled back and said, "I've wanted to do that since the panel discussion. It was all I could do to figure out how to be alone with you. I considered following you to the ladies' room when you slipped out but I opted for something a little more elegant."

Alberta's breath caught with excitement as she brushed Emma's dark curls back from her forehead and pulled her mouth back down to her own. The scent of Emma's sweat and the leather of her pants filled her head. Emma straddled Alberta's lap, pinning her against the back of the couch in a supple movement that didn't break their kiss. Alberta strained upward against Emma's weight, reaching out for the heat she felt.

"Lift," Emma said, shifting slightly off of Alberta. She reached down and tugged the linen skirt up Alberta's thighs. It slid softly on the nylon slip and stockings, bunching up around her waist. Alberta found herself worrying about the wrinkles. She had planned to wear the suit at her next engagement.

"There's always room service," Emma said, as if reading her mind. Again laughter surrounded them, making a bond that not even explicit knowledge could create as quickly.

Alberta's laughter turned to a gasp as she felt Emma's hand plunge inside of her stockings, then inside of her.

Emma sucked in Alberta's breath, kissing her deeply, searching out Alberta's tongue, while her hand moved inside her. Alberta pressed forward, loving the touch of Emma's mouth on hers. She drew back only to catch her breath, but Emma pursued her mouth, grasping her head with one hand. Her other pushed deeper inside.

"Oh, God! Alberta," Emma said, her voice full of disbelief.

She moved her hand gently for a moment. She kissed the side of

Alberta's face, her hair, her ear, finally resting her forehead on the sofa beside Alberta as all of her energy went through her hand into Alberta's body. She pushed hard, the full force of her inside of Alberta. Wetness deluged her fingers as she worked deeper. Alberta felt the desire like a tide wiping out all thought of anything else. The sound of Emma's voice took her higher, and left Liza behind. Alberta's voice was hoarse with desire.

They sat sprawled silently for many minutes, catching their breath. Alberta watched as Emma climbed over her. Alberta took in the soft texture of her skin and the musculature beneath the silk. The tape ended. Joan Armatrading's deep voice no longer masked their uneven breathing.

"Come," Emma said, standing in front of the couch, "we'll go back to your hotel. You can leave your suit to be pressed. I'll take you to the airport tomorrow."

"You really do think fast, don't you?"

"I had to have some kind of plan just in case you said yes. And you did say yes, didn't you." Emma pulled Alberta to her feet. Alberta noticed that without her heels she was not much taller than Emma; it made her want to hold Emma again. Less than an hour later they were curled around each other's bodies in the Holiday Inn.

The next day on the plane Alberta stared at the piece of notebook paper Emma had given her with her address and phone number, as if to assure herself she'd not dreamed the entire event. But it had not been a dream. Emma had been there in the morning when Liza called asking to take her to breakfast. Emma had discreetly showered while she and Liza almost had one of their familiar circuitous arguments when Alberta declined the invitation three times.

At the airport, Alberta and Emma had remembered they didn't know each other very well. Alberta hadn't been comfortable with the formality of giving Emma her card as they separated, but was grateful to have something impersonal to substitute for some other, more intimate expression.

Alberta went over her notes for her lecture that evening on women writers of the Harlem Renaissance and tried to push the encounter with Emma into the back of her mind. She'd never done anything like that before and never planned to again. But when she closed her eyes she could still feel the weight of Emma on her. The sensation stayed with Alberta throughout the rest of her trip. It remained with her after she was back home in Boston, and into the end of the semester.

Settled comfortably in the small booth of Bob the Chef's Restaurant, Alberta shoved her shopping bags under the table between her legs. Joyce did the same across from her, sweat gleaming on her caramel-colored forehead. Her tightly pressed hair was pulled back in a french twist, glistening under the bright lights of their old and familiar spot.

"I'll tell you, girl. I look at the figures and they just don't add up worth shit!"

Alberta always marveled at how quickly Joyce dropped the clipped tones she used at work in the insurance company and reverted to their Southern-tinged vernacular when they discussed their personal lives.

"I don't know what I'd do with her. Here, I mean."

"Don't they have a saying out there, 'I'm from Missouri, Show Me.' Seems like the girl done told you what to do with her. Here or anywhere!" Joyce had had the same mischievous sparkle since they were in high school together.

"She's twenty-five years old, Joyce!"

"She ain't asking you to adopt her!"

"She's, well, she's not black."

"I can only repeat myself."

They were silent as the waitress came and took their order.

"From what I gather, she's only five foot five, too. Maybe you better not have dinner with her."

They both smiled at that while Alberta tried to rephrase her objections.

"I just can't figure you out, Joyce. Why are you so hot on this? You never liked Liza."

"Hell, David didn't even like Liza."

Alberta looked at Joyce blankly.

"You remember David: forties, pretty skin, managed that auto body shop?"

"David wasn't on your dance card long enough to rate an opinion about my love life."

"What I'm saying is, Liza was trouble. Everybody, even David, could see that. And anybody who dares to be a lesbian and wear black leather pants in a Missouri college, anybody who sends you those cute Alison what's-her-name cartoon postcards...hell, anyone who can seduce you in the same state in which Elizabeth Bateson lurks, I like!"

Whenever Alberta questioned why she'd remained in Boston she always came up with Joyce as the answer. Since Alberta's mother died, Joyce had become her family—easy and tough at the same time. She had a distant cousin she knew still lived in the area, but Joyce was the one person she relied on.

"It's taken you over a year to get out from under Liza. Don't fall back on all those excuses. Either you like the girl or you don't. It's not like she's one of your students, or even goes to a school in the same state. Since you keep those postcards up on your fridge it looks like 'like' to me. And this entire conversation is moot until you start to have some of it with her."

"Well, maybe we can have drinks, or something."

"Is this some kind of lesbian dating ritual? Clue me in."

"She may not have much time. She's visiting some friends in Cambridge, so she might be tied up."

Joyce was silent.

"Okay, it can't hurt. She's incredibly bright and..." Alberta's voice sank into a whisper.

"Please don't start on that part—I can't bear to discuss sex when I'm eating chicken and dumplings."

The conversation with Joyce replayed itself in Alberta's head three weeks later as she waited in front of the "T" station on Massachusetts Avenue near Commonwealth. She wondered how she looked in her tan wool slacks and matching sweater. She'd given herself a haircut and was checking her rearview mirror when she felt Emma's presence beside her car.

Her heart leapt in her chest, but she leaned over casually to unlock the door. When Emma slid into the passenger's seat, Alberta

first trying to show intellect connect
cant lesbo relations just be hit + run

contrast w/ innocent blue

gazed at her dark blue eyes and couldn't remember why she'd been so afraid. Emma cupped Alberta's face in her hands and placed a tender kiss on her mouth.

"I"m so happy to see you. I can't tell you how happy. Only show you," Emma said.

Alberta laughed nervously, suddenly feeling shy. "I guess lunch can wait a while."

"No, lunch can't wait at all. Where do you live?" Emma answered, lowering her voice as she leaned into Alberta's ear to plant a small kiss on her neck.

Alberta made a U-turn on Massachusetts Avenue and drove smoothly back to the South End. Alberta was one of the few in her neighborhood who knew its history. She remembered the Hi Hat bar where her mother had been a barmaid. Nancy Wilson and Sarah Vaughn had stopped in during its heyday. She passed Charlie's sandwich shop. It now catered to investment bankers but used to be the neutral territory for ladies of the evening and the cops who worked the Columbus Avenue area.

By the time her mother had died, leaving the house to her, the night life of the South End had been shut down. Alberta had struggled to hold on to the house. She'd rented out rooms to other students like herself to avoid drowning under the wave of white professionals who'd discovered the crumbling South End and wanted to make it theirs.

She felt proud showing Emma around her house. Except for a few framed posters from her undergraduate days, all signs of student life were gone and the building was almost fully renovated.

"Is this where you and Elizabeth Bateson lived?"

"Shit!" Alberta said, then recovered herself. "She never lived here. She had a place in Cambridge. I guess college town talk is the same whether it's in Massachusetts or Missouri."

"There wasn't any talk, really. I knew that Prof. Bateson came out to Missouri from Boston University. Then the attitude she gave us as we were leaving, and the morning phone call, sort of made me think about it. When she dropped by the teaching assistants' office one evening and oh so casually asked me to stop for a drink with her, I knew she wanted something. She's never bothered to say more to me than hello, so it couldn't be purely professional. She's a bit of a bitch, I'd say."

"That's an understatement!"

Emma and Alberta both laughed.

"I want to make love to you. Now." The force of Emma's simple declaration flooded Alberta with warmth. She tried to remember, but was sure it had never been this uncomplicated for her.

They walked upstairs to the bedroom, bathed in bright afternoon light. Alberta draped her clothes carefully over an armchair she'd had covered in the wild print material that used to be her mother's curtains. She watched Emma step out of her jeans and toss her bright blue wool shirt onto the chair atop Alberta's tan outfit. When Alberta bent over the bed to pull back the comforter, Emma leaned against her back and pressed her down onto the bed. Alberta enjoyed the feel of Emma's hand as it caressed the contours of her back. The youthful strength felt alien and comfortable at the same time.

Emma kissed Alberta's neck, then slid down to kiss her back in repeated rows, back and forth, until she'd covered all of her skin. Alberta's breath came faster as Emma slid one hand down to spread Alberta's legs further apart.

"You know, I feel like I should go slowly. I want to go slowly. That will have to be later."

It was hours before they fell into a light sleep. The sun moved across the sky, leaving the room in a reddish glow before turning to darkness.

They woke many times, then finally slept deeply when the darkest part of night quieted the room and the city outside.

Alberta slipped from the bed in the morning and went down to the kitchen. She did her stretches in the parlor instead of the bedroom, trying to stay aware of each aching muscle. Every day she took inventory, listening to the way her body accumulated the years. Her feet, in particular, seemed to be less flexible. Today she could feel, in the ball of her hip joints, a new ache she was certain came from the energetic night before. Alberta tried to be gentle with each move but refused to go easy on herself.

Routine completed, she'd prepared tea and mixed a batch of quick cornbread before she heard Emma moving around in the bedroom upstairs. When she came down they sat enjoying breakfast. Their discussion of books and writing was as full of enthusiasm and as passionate as their lovemaking, but beyond that lay a shadowy gulf which each was unsure how to bridge. Alberta was casual and breezy, maintaining the space between them.

"This has been one of the most important experiences of my life," Emma said. "I have to say, though, that I feel a kind of disrespect from you. That's not exactly the word I want to use, but it's what comes out. I can tell you want to be with me even though there's this part of you that doesn't take me seriously, or something. Some kind of wall goes up as if you think I'm not worth the trouble. Maybe it means something else to you, but I can't really tell from this side."

"Disrespect has nothing to do with it. You don't realize what I've made of my life. You can't expect me to throw myself into something that doesn't even make sense to me. I don't know you."

"Do you want to? I get the feeling that if I hadn't had to be in town this weekend you never would have written or called me. Do you want to know me?"

"I don't know, Emma. Right now, I don't know."

Alberta saw the relief in Emma's eyes and felt terrible that she wasn't able to say more. Before she opened the door Alberta moved closer to Emma and reached out to touch her face. Emma pulled Alberta close and kissed her mouth. They held each other for a few minutes, then stepped out into the bright, late-morning sun.

"I see she's on to the 'Women Who Changed the World' postcards."

"Stop reading my mail, Joyce."

"When mail becomes refrigerator art it's public information." Joyce's trim body vibrated with humor.

"Whose rule is that?" Alberta started putting away the groceries she'd bought with Joyce on their monthly shopping expedition to the mall.

"Says she applied for jobs in Maryland and Massachusetts. And what did you say?" She tapped a newly manicured nail on the card.

"Nothing, yet."

"Yet? Girl, this card is a month old!"

"Will you *stop* that." Alberta snatched the card out of Joyce's hand and threw it on top of the refrigerator.

"Umm, Missouri seems to be slipping. Looks like the same post-card you had up the last time I was here. That girl sure got a way with words. Umph, umph, umph."

Alberta returned to the cabinet where she stored canned foods but said nothing.

"There ain't been this much dead air in here since what's-her-name left town. Maybe you better spit it out before it gets much later in the evening."

"I hate when you do that, Joyce. Her name is Elizabeth—"

"Okay, okay. Don't try to change my direction. What's on your mind, or should I be asking, what's up in Missouri?"

"I'm thinking of going out there to visit her."

"Thinking?"

"Well, I've got a reservation for a flight. I might or might not use it. I don't know yet."

"Correct me if I'm wrong, but didn't we have a similar conversation earlier this spring? Girl, I can't spend my time repeating myself."

Alberta was silent. Sometimes Joyce's abrupt style and keen intuition made her angry. She felt exposed and juvenile, agonizing over an idea Joyce had already so easily analyzed and dispatched. She kept working, ignoring Joyce's penetrating stare, then raked her fingers through her short, dark hair and gazed at the digital timer on the oven as if it were an instrument for forecasting the future.

"Let me cut to the chase for you. You made these reservations and you're afraid to go because she might reject you, or worse, might be thrilled to see you and that would mean you have to respond in some responsible way, like admitting you adore her and want to make more of it. How am I doing so far?"

Alberta said nothing.

"And then there's what's-her-name, your ex, who will probably be lurking in the bush so that she's certain to witness whatever happens between you and Emma and assure that it makes the six o'clock news, preferably national. Then the bank will call in your mortgage on this house. Your few remaining relatives, whom you seldom speak to, will disinherit you. And the last but certainly not least of the retributions: I, your oldest friend, will find you ridiculous and dump you."

Joyce stopped, hoping to hear laughter from Alberta. Instead there was silence. When she looked closely she saw tears forming under Alberta's closed lashes.

"Oh baby, I'm sorry, I didn't mean to make you cry. You got it all backward. I know all those other things are scary, but you can't be afraid of trying again. You remember Frank?"

"Frank?"

"Yeah, kinda tall, curly dark hair, blue eyes, I met him at that branch manager's conference."

"What about him?"

"Well, when he and I broke up, I didn't feel no worse than I did with anybody else. Pissed off is pissed off."

"Joyce, what are you talking about?"

"I'm just saying, I don't think a white girl can break your heart anymore than anybody else can! Take it slow if you want, but don't just walk away because it don't fit your picture."

"When she was here and we were having tea here at this table..." Alberta looked around the kitchen, then sat down as if all the energy had drained from her. "...I looked up over there...my mother's old coffee pot. We've had that since I was a kid." Alberta wiped her face on the sleeve of her sweatshirt. "I've got dishes that are older than that girl, Joyce. I don't think I can handle that."

"You know what I think it is? Not her being young. It's you being old. I got it now!"

Alberta laughed.

"Laugh if you want, but that's the real deal. We're hitting that age...the change...and you're afraid."

"When Liza left me, I couldn't imagine the future without her. I still can't."

"You're in the middle of your future, Alberta, come on. Ain't you the one told me lesbians are always young. Come on! Your life sure didn't stop when Professor Liza left you. I think you've done a few things for yourself here. And none of it looks like digging a grave."

"When she's touching me I can feel how much time she's got in front of her and I want to cry. My body feels like...like a sweatsuit, Joyce. I'm a sweatsuit, she's leather pants."

"What are you talking about? You're in better shape than any-body from our neighborhood, except me. And I know you can move with the best of 'em."

"What do I do when I hate her because she's at the beginning of her life and I'm not, huh? She's a kid."

"How old?"

"Maybe twenty-five."

"Correct me if I'm wrong, but by that time hadn't we done a lot of adult living? Did we or did we not sit in at the Provost's office in 1969 until they took us to jail? Did we or did we not go after those guys in Dorchester with tire irons when they kept driving by your girlfriend's apartment yelling 'dyke'? We faced enough adult living by the time we were twenty-five to be insulted at being called a kid."

Joyce moved closer to Alberta and took her hands in hers.

"Come on. We survived '50s television: you're not going to let a little healthy desire scare you, are you?"

Finally, Joyce heard a soft giggle.

"We're getting older, Alberta, no question. But that's the good news, girlfriend."

"I keep wondering if I'd had a child if I wouldn't feel so afraid."

"Don't go back there. I sat up with you for hours on that, okay? I know more than I want to about insemination and donors and all that. Please. You considered, you decided. That's not what this is about. Liza was your big romance, your life partner, like you kept saying. But she wasn't. That's it. And that don't mean you're old and your life is over. I'm the same age and I know mine ain't over."

"She sees the world like some big...I don't know. Something she's just going to dig into and take what's hers."

"Isn't that what we wanted to happen for women? Don't begrudge her the optimism you fought for."

"She's—"

"From what you said she didn't get anything dropped into her lap. She worked hard."

"She's done wonderfully. I think she's the first in her family to get a college degree."

"So she's not just looking at the world like a big something she's digging into."

"That's not what I meant..."

"Her energy feels too optimistic. Makes you feel old. I'm telling you that's it. So I think you need to grab onto some of it."

Alberta was talked out. She kept thinking she had more to say, but each thought seemed to lead back to an answer Joyce had already devised. Instead she said, "It's an afternoon flight."

"I'll take you to the airport just like I did the first time you went out of town for a speaking gig. Remember how we got drunk in the airport bar at 10:00 A.M.? Come on."

"Two weeks from tomorrow. I haven't let Emma know I want to come yet."

"I'll take the day off in case I get a hangover."

Alberta came down the corridor of the St. Louis airport acutely aware that hers was one of the few black faces in the wave of rumple-suited businessmen disembarking from the plane. She carried a week-ender bag and her briefcase as if they had no weight at all, keeping her shoulders even and her head high. She spotted Emma scanning the crowd and smiled when she ran toward her. Alberta turned over her bag, happy to have something to do in the first awkward moment. She could kiss her, crush her in her arms, but that felt too familiar, at odds with the space still between them.

The ride home was quick, filled with questions and answers about Emma's thesis. They sat at the kitchen table and Emma served Alberta the glass of juice which she requested to wash down a couple of aspirins.

"It's just a little headache, it'll be gone in a while."

Emma sat anxiously watching Alberta's face. Looking for signs of something, she decided to wait before taking up any serious conversation.

"My best friend Joyce and I have a little ritual that involves a lot of drinking. Whenever I have to do anything tough or new."

"Like what?"

"Like the first time I went off to do a lecture at Berkeley twenty years ago and I was terrified. Like coming out here to see you and tell you how I feel."

Emma rose abruptly from the kitchen table and went to the re-frigerator to refill her glass.

Alberta gazed at Emma's back, feeling a rush of tenderness and desire. She sensed Emma's anxiety and it mirrored her own, which had hung over her life since the summer. But even stronger than her fear was the certainty that she could not live in limbo forever. If Liza was out of her life, Alberta knew she had to figure out what her life would look like. It had hit Alberta when she spotted Emma running toward her at the airport—her strong, athletic sprint, the way her curls flew around her face and her eyes shone with joy and nervous-ness—that she wanted to start by getting to know who Emma was.

"I have to make a confession which I guess will say it all." Alberta watched Emma's face as she returned to the table.

"I am not on my way to Stanford to do a lecture. I was lying about that because I was afraid to just arrive...myself...here to see you. I thought it'd be easier, more casual, if it were just a stop on the way somewhere. Then neither of us would have to act like it was a big deal. I just wanted to see you..."

Alberta stopped when she saw Emma was trying to restrain a smile. Then Emma's laughter burst into the room around them. She doubled over, at first frightening Alberta into thinking she'd been completely wrong about how Emma felt.

"You have to stop. Wait...wait." Emma gulped, trying to regain her composure.

"I have to tell you about this winter...when I came to Boston to see you. I don't have any friends in Cambridge. I just came for you. So I got a hotel room and pretended to be going somewhere so you wouldn't think I was forcing myself on you."

"What!"

"I made up the friends and all, just to—"

"Hold up a minute." Alberta tried to pull her thoughts together. She could see wariness descend in Emma's eyes.

"I know you care about me quite a bit," Alberta reasssured her.

"Why do I feel like I'm not going to be happy?"

"I haven't been fair with you, Emma, and I want to because you mean a lot to me, too."

Emma got up from the table and paced the room.

"This is the first relationship or anything for me since Liza left. 'Dumped me' I guess is more accurate. I still don't have a good sense of myself. I know I feel great when I'm with you, but I want you to understand—I just don't know anything else for sure."

"How could you?"

"I can't. But you're sure. Right now you think this is going to be bliss. We're meant for each other. Nothing else matters to you."

"Condescension is not your most romantic mode, Alberta."

"We can't pretend that we're not in different places. Desire won't cover that over forever. I'm still hurting from Liza and I don't bounce back as quickly as I did twenty years ago. Our actions don't have the same consequences, Emma."

Emma sat back down in the kitchen chair, her lips pursed as she tried to let Alberta's words in.

"Are you telling me to be careful?"

"I'm telling you I'm no earth mother goddess. I'm scared to do this. What if we both think we're too cool to worry about race and we end up hurting each other? I'm almost ready to retire. You're just starting. How soon before that comes between us? I'm scared of all that, Emma. Despite what you think you see, I've never been much of a risk-taker."

"I promise—"

"There's no such thing as a promise."

Alberta paced the kitchen, not looking at Emma.

"Maybe not, but I'm saying it anyway: If this doesn't work, whatever that means, I promise not to let what happened with you and Liza happen with us."

"You can't promise that."

"I can promise to treat you with respect. And if one of us screws up we can promise to try to learn something from it. We can promise to try to forgive whatever ghosts we stir up. I can promise to keep what we care about special: the writers, the politics. I can promise that. Don't dismiss those things like Liza Bateson did when she left."

However she looked at it, Alberta felt like a lion was nipping at her heels and she was about to step off a cliff. Her fear of broken bones was as sharp as the terror in standing still. Alberta nodded and let Emma lead her upstairs to the bedroom she'd not seen before.

They made love to each other through the afternoon and into the night. They finally drifted into sleep holding one another close, perspiration building up on their skin where it touched. When Alberta opened her eyes she found Emma leaning up on her elbow, watching her.

"It's almost ten o'clock. How about some food?"

"Good idea. May I use the telephone first?"

"Sure," Emma said, puzzled. She pulled the phone up from the floor and sat it on the bed. She started to rise and move away, but Alberta held on to her leg. With the other hand she punched the buttons briskly.

"Hi, Joyce, it's me. Yeah, yeah I'm here. Listen, I want to make a dinner date. I'm cooking. Just a minute."

Alberta turned to Emma. "So when can you get to Boston next?"

She turned back to the phone. "How about Saturday, October 18th, 7:00 P.M.?" Alberta giggled low.

"You can bring the wine. We prefer white, and none of that cheap shit you got to water down to make it stay down. Alright, see ya."

Emma looked at Alberta quizzically.

"Joyce is my best friend since high school. High femme, straight girl. A lot of things I might not have survived without her—my mother dying, getting my degree, Liza leaving. Getting here today. So you want me, you get her." ✦

PIECE OF TIME

*V*eda kneeled down to reach behind the toilet, her pink cotton skirt pulled tight around her brown thighs. Her skin already glistened with sweat from the morning sun and her labors. She moved quickly through the hotel room, sanitizing tropical mildew and banishing sand. Each morning our eyes would meet in the mirror just as she wiped down the tiles and I raised my arms in a last wake-up stretch after tea. I once imagined that her gaze flickered over my body, enjoying my broad, brown shoulders, or catching a glance of my plum brown nipples as the large African cloth in which I was wrapped dropped away to the floor. The thought startled me at first. Then I'd had a fleeting sense of the pristine hardness of the bathroom tiles at my back and her damp skin pressed against mine, and I flushed with secret embarrassment.

"Okay, it's finished here," Veda said as she folded the cleaning rag and hung it in the cabinet under the sink. She turned around and seemed surprised that I was still watching her. Her eyes were light brown and didn't quite hide their smile; her dark, straightened hair was tied back with a ribbon. The ponytail hung lightly on her neck the way that straightened hair does. My own was in short tight braids that brushed my shoulders, a colored bead at the end of each. It was a trendy affectation I'd indulged in for my vacation.

I smiled. She smiled back. On a trip filled with so much great food, music, and new faces, the flash of Veda's grin was what I looked for each morning. That surprised me, too. It was like she was my best friend, yet we hardly knew each other. Something in the inquisitive smile which fought the reserve in her eyes drew me.

She gathered the towels from the floor, opening the hotel room door in the same motion.

"Good-bye."

"See ya," I said, feeling about twelve years old instead of thirty. She shut the door softly behind her, and I listened to the clicking of her silver bangle bracelets as she walked around the verandah toward the stairs. My room was the last one on the second level facing the beach. Her bangles brushed the painted wood railing as she went down, then crossed the tiny courtyard to the front office.

I dropped my cloth to the floor and stepped into my bathing suit. I planned to swim for hours and lie in the sun reading and sipping pina coladas until I could do nothing but sleep. I'd almost had to threaten suicide to get this time off; I knew it was not a completely idle threat. The tight, angry faces I looked into every day on the Metro, making my way to work, were mirrored at my office once I arrived. I'd known that working as a paralegal would not be a source of sparkling conversation and witty camaraderie, but each year it became more difficult to endure the patently false smiles that passed for worker relations in a law firm.

[margin note: Super job once again]

Five years after starting there, I kept hoping some sincerity or human warmth might slip in. But I felt, for the most part, completely unseen. How a black person with a full-time job could feel invisible in an almost all-black city remained a mystery to me. At work I was simply an efficient, personable functionary, a paid employee who didn't register on the partners' human Richter scale. With friends I was just an unmarried black woman who, they thought, acted too hincty to ever get a man. If I didn't know I had lunch twice a week with Randy, the other black paralegal on the sixth floor, I'd wonder if I really existed. I decided to send him a postcard, just

[margin note: shows prejud w/in blk comm]

[margin note: always close one friend]

to have a way of making sure.

One vacation day turned languidly into another, each closer to my return to the city and the job. I didn't dread going home; it felt almost as if home wouldn't be there when I got back. Here, time didn't seem to move in the same way. I could prolong any pleasure until I had my fill, then pack my bags, fly home, and something completely different would be there when I landed. The luxury of the island was a fantasy from my childhood—a tiny neighborhood gone to sea. The music of the language, the fresh smells and deep colors enveloped me. I clung to the bosom of this place. All else disappeared.

Early one morning, before her time to begin work in the rooms, Veda passed below in the courtyard carrying a bag of laundry. She deposited the bundle in a bin, then returned. I called down to her, my voice whispering in the cool, private morning air, and raised my cup of tea in invitation when she looked up. As she turned in from the beach end of the courtyard, I prepared another cup.

We stood together at the door, she more out than in, talking about fishing and the rain storm of two days previous and how we'd spent Christmas.

Soon she said, "I'd better be getting to my rooms."

"I'm going to swim this morning," I said.

"Then I'll be coming in now, all right? I'll do the linen," she said, and began to strip the bed. I went into the bathroom and turned on the shower.

When I stepped out and opened the door to let the steam escape I saw the bed was fresh, its covers snapped firmly around the corners. The sand was swept from the floor tiles back outside, and our tea cups were put away. I knelt to rinse the tub.

"No, I do that. I'll do it, please."

She came toward me, a look of alarm on her face. I laughed. She reached for the cleaning rag in my hand as I bent over the suds, then she laughed, too. As I knelt on the edge of the tub, my cloth came unwrapped and fell in. We both tried to retrieve it from the draining water. My feet slid on the wet tiles and I sat down on the floor with a thud.

"Are you hurt?" she said, holding my cloth in one hand, reaching out to me with the other. She looked only into my eyes. Her hand was soft and firm on my shoulder as she knelt down. I watched the line of the muscles in her forearm, then traced the soft inside with my hand. She exhaled slowly, her warm breath brushing my face as she bent closer. I pulled her down and pressed my mouth to hers. There was no preparation; the act was the thought. My tongue pushed between her teeth, gently at first. I didn't know what to expect, but my body seemed to.

Her arms encircled my shoulders. We lay back on the tiles, her body atop mine. She removed her cotton T-shirt. Her brown breasts were nestled insistently against me. I raised my leg between hers. The moistness that matted the hair there dampened my leg. Her body moved in a brisk and demanding rhythm.

I wondered briefly if the door was locked, but wanted to assume it was. I heard Veda call my name for the first time. I stopped her with my lips. Her hips were searching, pushing toward their goal. Veda's mouth on mine was sweet and full with hungers of its own.

Her right hand held the back of my neck and her left hand found its way between my thighs, brushing the hair and flesh softly at first, then playing over the outer edges. Her hand moved back and forth. A gasp escaped my mouth and I opened my legs wider, wedging us between the basin and the sink. Her finger slipped past the soft outer lips and entered me so tenderly, at first I didn't feel it. Then she pushed inside and I felt myself open. I tried to swallow my scream of pleasure. Veda's tongue filled my mouth and sucked up my joy. We lay still for a moment, our breathing and the seagulls the only sound.

She pulled herself up.

"Miss—" she started.

I cut her off again, this time my fingers to her lips. "I think it's okay if you stop calling me Miss!"

"Carolyn," she said softly, again covering my mouth with hers. We kissed for moments that wrapped around us, making time have no meaning. She exhaled, the air trembling from her, then she rose. "It gets late, you know," she said with a smile.

She pulled away, her determination not yielding to my need. "I have my work, girl. I'll see you later. Not tonight, I see my boyfriend on Wednesdays. I got to go."

She brushed my lips with her fingers and was out the door. I lay back on the tile floor and listened to her bangles as she ran down the stairs.

On the beach that afternoon my skin still tingled, and the sun pushed my temperature higher. I stretched out on the deck chair with my eyes closed. I felt her mouth, her hands, and the sun on me, and came again.

I awoke with a start, thinking for a moment I'd dreamed the whole thing. But my body was in a state of languor usually precipitated only by making love.

Veda arrived each morning. There were only five left. She tapped lightly, then entered. I would look up from the small table where I'd prepared tea. She sat and we sipped slowly; then we slipped into the bed. We made love, sometimes gently, other times with a roughness resembling the waves that crashed the sea wall below.

When there was time, we talked. Her boyfriend, who was married, saw her only once or twice a week. She worked at two jobs, saving money to buy land, maybe on this island or on her home island. We were the same age, and although my life seemed to contain the material things she was still striving for, it was I who felt rootless and undirected.

We talked of our families, hers dependent on her help, mine so proud of me, and each of us still uncertain how we fit into their expectations. We shared our tales of growing up, the paths that led us to the same but different places. She loved this island. I did too. She could stay. I could not.

We didn't talk about "us," what it meant that two women were giving each other pleasure. I tried to imagine her in my life back home even though I could barely picture myself there any longer. One more self-aggrandizing partners' meeting or flashy, vacuous cocktail party and I was sure to run amok. It wasn't like I carried a list of current international events in my purse, hoping to bring them up. But my friends, the men I dated, and co-workers exhibited a level of disconnection from the world (other than the stock market) that was making me increasingly irritable, as if my life were unraveling and I couldn't pick up the stitch.

The term *colonialism* might not roll naturally off Veda's tongue, but she knew it when she saw it. She talked about the people in her town who worked in luxury hotels and had to take turns at home having running water.

On the third morning of the five I said, "You could visit me, come to the city for a vacation or..."

"And what I'm goin' to do there?"

I was angry but not sure if it was at her for refusing to drop everything and take a chance, or at myself for not accepting the sea that existed between us.

I felt narrow and self-indulgent in my desire for her. The ugly American—black but still acting like everything I'd always despised. Yet I wanted to be with her. I couldn't remember feeling such urgency in a long time.

The day before I'd left on vacation I'd gone out to lunch with a couple of women from another firm and they had practically salivated when I told them about my trip. Their focus was less on the sun and surf and more on available men. "Girl, they're just waiting down there for American black girls on the loose. All you got to do is hang out and look good."

I'd laughed as if that were my plan, when in my head I could only think how much it sounded exactly like what I did every weekend in D.C. It was like putting myself together in a neat package and popping onto a conveyer belt to wait for a man to claim me, as if I were a lost item. And I knew that each of the women, laughing like they were talking about striking gold, did the same thing. Then complained on Monday when they were still sitting in the Lost and Found.

More than once I'd called one of them on a Saturday afternoon to see if they'd like to go to a movie and they rushed me off the phone, keeping the lines clear just in case a date materialized. The first time I didn't get it. By the third and fourth time, however, I figured I might as well take myself to the movies. On Mondays when I'd ask, Did he call?, most of them said no as if it didn't matter. I couldn't imagine Veda ever twisting herself up into that kind of knot. And I began to feel my own knots coming loose.

I couldn't imagine myself going to lunch with the girls and telling them about Veda, but I tried.

The next morning I was up at dawn, puzzling through my feel-ings. They seemed both alien and natural at the same time, yet they were as clear as anything I'd ever experienced. I started to go outside and walk on the beach. I felt too unsteady, though, not collected enough to be in public, even before daylight. I paced my room as if the floor was hot, unable to be still, uncomfortable with every move. I finally sat down at the table, thinking I could make a list; that often helped me sort things out. Veda found me with my head on my arms, asleep. The small shopping bag I usually saw her carry to work and deposit in a locker downstairs every morning sat on the floor by the door.

"Should I come back?" she asked in a tentative voice that straddled both our worlds—housekeeper and guest.

"Can we talk a minute?"

"We're good at that, too," she said with a smile.

She started to prepare the tea, but I stopped her. "No, I get to wait on you, remember?"

I was uncertain what it was I needed to say.

"Do you ever worry about your boyfriend's wife finding out about you two?"

"Ach, she knows. It works out."

"What does that mean?"

"She knows I don't want her husband. Just someone to go around with every once in a while. She the one want babies, not me."

"Don't you want to get married?" I'd never elevated matrimony to a state of grace, so I could barely believe the word was in my mouth.

"Maybe, when I'm old. Right now, it's not time to listen to some-one telling me what to do."

I laughed at the direct way she dismissed the elemental quality of marriage I'd never been able to articulate.

"I just never did this before. I don't know what to do next."

"Why you need to know about next? What about now?"

"Now, I'm about as happy as a sleepy, hungry woman can be."

"I know you going home soon. Don't get worried over that."

"Not worried, Veda. Sad. Who'll I make tea for?"

"You'll find some little lawyer. Maybe one of those computer girls you say help you learn how to work them when you first start up."

It came out so easily—*girls*—as if it was natural. I felt both sad and exhilarated at the same time.

"Don't be looking at me so. Life goin' on all the time."

It was as if she were deliberately keeping us on our different sides of the ocean. "What about you?" I asked.

"Girls together all the time here. Nobody worried 'til it look too serious. I got my family to think of."

I glanced at the little travel clock. "Don't fret," Veda said. "I called in sick today. We got dinner in my bag."

I packed up fruit from the small room refrigerator, and we snuck down the back stairs of the hotel, keeping out of sight of the front office. We settled on the beach.

"All you come down here to burn up in the sun. I need my shade," Veda said, laughing, as she raised a beach umbrella.

We read magazines, napped, and talked. Except for the current of desire that wafted across our skin with the breeze, the afternoon was completely peaceful. We stayed together until the sun was almost set. Then it was time for her to get home and help with her sister's children so she could go to work on the night shift of the casino in town. The next day I sat in the same spot on the beach, feeling the sand hot beneath me as I imagined Veda's body heat, knowing it was only the sun.

On my last night of vacation, after packing, I sat up with a bottle of wine listening to the waves beneath my window and the tourist voices from the courtyard. Veda tapped at my door as I was thinking of going to bed. When I opened it she came inside quickly and thrust an envelope and a small gift-wrapped box into my hand.

"Can't stay, you know. He waiting down there. I'll be back in the morning." I held her arm. "This is my life in a small place, not some dirty big city." Then she pulled away and ran out and down the stairs before I could respond.

Early in the morning she entered with her key. I was awake but lying still. She was out of her clothes and beside me in a moment. Our lovemaking began abruptly but built slowly. We touched each part of our bodies, imprinting memories on our fingertips.

"I don't want to leave you," I whispered.

"You're not leaving me. Just I must stay here." She stopped and looked around the room. "Maybe you'll write to me. Maybe you'll come back. Who knows."

I started to speak, but she quieted me.

"Don't make words now, girl. We make love."

Her hands on me and inside of me pushed the city away. My mouth eagerly drew in the flavors of her body. We lay with each other as if the trip had just begun. We slept only a few moments before it was time for her to dress and go on with her chores.

"I'll come back to ride with you to the airport?" she said with a small question mark at the end.

"Yes," I said, pleased.

"Good, kiss me now then." We held each other, saying the good-bye we could not say in public later. She finally leaned away and our breath filled the air between us. She slipped out the door. I spent an hour sitting on the balcony gazing out at the ocean, marveling at how different we were from each other, yet how much alike we were, and trying to recall what back home looked like now. Images collaged through my head but nothing came into a sharp focus. Not to remember the place I lived in didn't frighten me. Maybe it'd be new by the time I arrived. I snapped my suitcase shut. The bright cloth I'd wrapped myself in every morning was still slightly damp from washing; it was folded neatly on the small kitchen table beside my note for Veda.

In the airport's tiny waiting room I sat fingering the gift Veda had given me: a silver charm bracelet with a tiny tea cup.

"It fits then."

I was afraid to speak. Veda took out a small photo album and started showing me pictures of her mother, sisters, nieces, and nephews. I wanted to scream. Instead I listened to the musical softness of her voice and looked at the pictures of the people who were her world. In some of the faces I could see her eyes or mouth. Sometimes the snapshot showed a relative with an arm thrown easily around Veda's waist, or a friend balanced playfully on her lap. I stared into the faces as if their mouths would open and they'd speak to me.

"See, see, this one." Veda pointed to a young girl of about eleven.

"She gonna be like you. I can tell that now. I'll send you her picture."

"What do you mean?" The girl had dark eyebrows that shadowed her lively eyes and bore no resemblance to me at all.

"You mark me, she gonna be like you. Fresh!" Veda winked at me and laughed loud enough to turn the heads of others waiting in the tiny airport. "Maybe she'll be a lawyer too. Look in her face, see?"

We sat together waiting for the announcement of my plane as if we'd done it many times before, never mentioning tomorrow morning. She looked at me more directly than anyone I'd known in the past ten years. I looked back at Veda and actually saw something there to hold on to.

When she kissed my cheek, she whispered *sister-love* in my ear, so softly I wasn't sure I'd heard it until I searched her eyes. I held her close for only a moment, wanting more. I boarded the plane, and time began to move again. ✦

Pattern of stories
typical

Experimenting
similar to vacation?

LYNX AND STRAND

Until the day that you are me and I am you...
I'll be loving you always.
—Stevie Wonder

As she walked through the door, twin reflections of the firm set of her back moved closer together in the corner of the restaurant window. The images converged in the mirrored panes of glass and vanished inside each other like chips of colored crystal in a kaleidoscope. Across the street a bland shadow stepped from a doorway and followed. Strand's heart thudded, she gulped for breath.

"Whoa!" Nelson said in his soft voice, easing Strand out of her reverie. The shadow receded. Strand opened her eyes and recognized Nelson's living room, edged with twilight, encircling the beam of a stark lamp focused on her. Strand, laying on her stomach on the waist-high massage table, struggled to let go of the memory and the fear inside it.

"Sorry. I was just remembering something."

"You want to sit up a minute?"

"No, let's just go."

He held out her glass with its bent straw and green liquid. She shook her head, turning onto her other cheek, and gazed at Nelson's heavily laden bookcase.

"I go. You stay still." Nelson balanced between the heels and balls of his feet. He kept his considerable weight centered so that he barely leaned forward over the expanse of Strand's back. For eleven months they'd spent hours in this way: Strand listening to the past unreeling in her head as Nelson worked on her. Other times they'd told each other stories, true and untrue. Under the spell of their words the tattoo took shape almost independently. Now, as they neared the end of the project, both were increasingly anxious. Conversation came in choppy swells, uneven and unfinished, without the certainty Strand enforced in most of her life.

"What're you thinking about?"

"Work," Strand lied.

"And?"

Strand pushed the shadow to the back and cast about for news to share. "Did I tell you about the dancing potato chip guy? If I ever have another client like him, I'll leap from the tower window before we're done."

"They don't open," Nelson responded, never letting his gaze waver from her back.

"Then I'll smash it."

"You don't like heights."

"I won't know, will I?"

"It'd be messy. Your secretary, Freda, would have to clean up after you."

"You want to hear or not," she continued. The hum of Nelson's machine and its vibrating needles remained steady. "He had the stupidest concept I've ever heard. These chips hoofing it around the edge of a volcano, like they're about to hop in and get fried."

"Please don't make me laugh, okay?"

"But the thing was, he kept insisting we go on location. He wanted to go out West! I told him Mount St. Helens is no joke, that I wasn't balancing some dumb and desperate dancers on the edge of a volcano when I could do it in a simuroom."

"Bet Broadcast loved him."

"He had this deep voice he kept throwing around like it was a police stick. 'You don't understand,' he says to me, 'this isn't a matter of your artistic whim, this is government advertising in Society City.'"

Nelson tried to hold steady and not laugh at Strand's imitation.

"So I say, 'No, this is advertising on the far coast and I won't go!' I dumped the job. I couldn't work with this slób. He's had one thought his entire life and this was it."

"Damn, Strand, you're rough." Nelson's voice was mixed with admiration and wariness.

"There are plenty of other commercialists at the company hungry for the work. Why waste my time with dancing potato chips?"

"Strand," Nelson said, trying to keep the judgment out of his voice, hating this brittle side of her.

"Broadcast doesn't really like to go past the Cities, anyway. So end of story, right? Uh-uh. Today Freda said somebody in Tech told her this guy did end up going out there. I don't know if he got as far as Washington, but out he goes with a crew, you know."

Strains of laughter began to bubble up from her stomach.

"Okay, I can feel a break coming on." Nelson stepped back and let his machine arm rest at his side.

"So, he sets off, right, with a crew...I'm sorry." Strand was almost enveloped in laughter. "He goes out there...forest...unpaved...the whole untamed nature thing and...," Strand raised herself up on her elbows, "and...he gets himself killed!" Her laughter pealed like a bell.

"Killed, how?" A chill crossed Nelson's skin.

"Who knows. One of the tech crew said separatists probably booby-trapped the location. They found him practically disemboweled in some woods—"

"That's not funny, Strand."

"Shit, he was an ad man."

"And they haven't called themselves separatists in decades. They're Partisans. Why do they get blamed for everything?"

"Relax."

"You relax!" Nelson snapped, surprised by his impatience. "Don't dismiss people so easy."

"He was just—"

"He was just a person."

Both were quiet, an unnatural state between them, until Nelson spoke.

"They keep telling us Partisans are raving lunatics, ready to kill anybody outside the perimeters of the Cities. Why, Strand? Why keep us away from the old places. Away from people trying to hang on to some integrity."

Strand had never heard Nelson so upset, certainly not with her. "Think, Strand! That's supposed to be your claim to fame."

She stared at his books, not seeing their titles. At Broadcast One there was an endless static of voices—technicians, producers, advertisers, directors like herself. She'd learned to let clients babble while she thought about their concepts, examining them from all angles until she perceived the image she wanted. Then she matched the rhythms and tone of the conversation, pitching her voice above it and off-center just enough to capture their attention. As she waited for the space to step into, her face looked much as it did now: a store shuttered and closed for the night.

Strand had once caught herself in the glass window of her tower office. She had seen that look reflected back, superimposed on the small world below, her mouth set in a hard line which she never broke until a client hired her. For her thoughts, her ideas.

"I correct myself. Don't think, Strand. Feel."

She leaned up for the glass of tranq, sipped, and lowered herself back to the table. When Nelson clicked the machine back on, she shuddered and drifted away from his words. She didn't want to think or feel. Instead she savored the image of him hovering over her body just like he did when he worked in the art class they took together.

Cardarelli, the instructor, whispered apologetically in class when she made suggestions over a painter's shoulder, moving about the room, always avoiding Strand who became enraged by interruption. Strand enjoyed the small island each easel created and the hushed atmosphere of concentration. She took the class as required by Professional Development, but PD couldn't make her listen to an instructor if she chose otherwise. With merely a glance Strand was able to decipher, analyze, or reproduce any image put before her. She hadn't needed instruction in art since she'd left the orphanage at fifteen.

"I'm taking a stretch break," Nelson said after a few moments, flipping the switch on the machine. "You want something?"

"No. How much longer do you think?"

"A month, maybe. I'm doing a second layer of colors now."

"It's like we've known each other forever, you know that."

"Except we keep knowing something new."

"Um."

"How's Lynx doing?"

"Good. A lot better, really." Strand thought about what that meant: Lynx was able to sleep without drugs. She could be in a room with more than one person without being sedated.

"I want her to come by soon."

"She will, it's just hard for her when she gets off her shift."

"Soon, though." Nelson splayed his palms together, pushing and flexing. He brushed Strand's forehead gently with his fingertips, then dropped forward at the waist, his large bulk in its dark caftan filling the space beside her. He stretched noisily and squatted next to Strand, his brown face even with hers. His large dark eyes and sleekly arched eyebrows were accentuated by the stark beauty of his bald head.

"You know I'm going to miss you when we're done," he said, and was startled to see tears forming in the corner of her eyes. He turned away, gripped the edge of the lounge, and did two half push-ups.

"Hell, you'll be happy to have more time to hang out at Ruby's," she replied. Then, more softly, as if barely saying it made it barely true, "You and Lynx are the only people in the world I love."

"There'll soon be a lot more."

"If they don't stop us." It was unusual for Strand to express uncertainty.

"They think it's just an art project. They won't care."

"They care about everything—the trains running on time and real tattoos."

Working at Broadcast, Strand saw how closely the government monitored every nuance of public social interaction, from street crime to who bought "adult" music. Strand didn't underestimate the Society's investment in any of its citizens.

"The Joneses," Nelson said with disgust.

The Joneses was Nelson's epithet for the Society and its privatized bureaucracy. The federal government was composed of intricately linked, regional oversight committees with profit and order in mind. They strategized how many workers needed education, which citizens had run out of their right to public assistance, what types of artists needed stimulation, and, most importantly, which television producers and directors said what over the national channels. The Joneses.

"Back to work if you can stand it."

"I'm just imagining we're in Cardarelli's studio class and I'm the canvas."

Nelson rubbed his hands vigorously around his smooth head as if gathering the thoughts that were inside, then took the machine in hand. Pinned to the walls around them were the drawings he'd done of Lynx in that class, and others he'd done of Strand over the six years they'd known each other. He was always looking for the life behind the images. With this tattoo, he'd found it.

Strand herself was usually more interested in affect, her meticulous eye taking in content only tangentially. During her years living in the Society North Orphanage, Strand had learned to watch the shapes of things to discern meaning. The floor supervisor's arched eyebrow let her know what was safe to say. The angle of the door to the principal's office informed her of how severe her punishment would be. A child's curving lip said she'd refuse to talk to the tall, awkward Strand. The act of deciphering these signs became its own meaning; whatever occurred subsequently had been almost inconsequential to Strand the child. She'd lived for symbols and surfaces until two years ago, when Lynx arrived to model for their class.

Lynx stepped up onto the platform, a large crocheted hat crowning her nudity. Kneeling ceremoniously, she drew the hat back from her forehead, releasing a mass of tawny orange hair emblazoned with streaks of pure silver to cascade down her back and around her breasts. A collective gasp swept around the studio as they recognized the silver marks of an empath. Cardarelli beamed with pride. She was the first instructor at the Institute, in the entire city, to have secured an empath as a model. Most of the students had never met one, although they'd certainly heard of the social services the E Corps performed for the Society in hospitals and detention centers.

Strand forced herself to look away from the mesmerizing tangle of hair, which Lynx made no effort to tame. Strand focused instead on the body, just as she did with clients when their voices got in her way. This one was short, athletic, the arms thick with muscle, a body altogether at odds with the mass of bright, delicate tendrils. The skin, unexpectedly, was not just freckled but bronzed from the sun. Despite their fine bones, her hands looked like those of a toiler, bearers of many heavy loads. Everything about Lynx seemed both small and large at the same time. The set of mismatched attributes was puzzling to Strand. Even in recline, Lynx seemed to fill the room.

Strand didn't begin to look at Lynx's face until the end of the first week. She spent all her time trying to read her body: the flare of hip from her waist, the texture of skin and the fine hairs that covered it. Near the end of the week Strand realized that Lynx, unlike most models, sat perfectly still. The curve of her muscle was stony hard beneath the flesh. For hours she sat, as if all life were suspended. The only movement was that of her hair, blown occasionally by a current from the forced-air vent. Strand became curious about the concentration at the center of the icy stillness. There were no clues in Lynx's face. Her features remained impassive, the bright hazel of her eyes almost opaque. The shield masking Lynx's gaze annoyed Strand at first. Her job was about surfaces, but here she wanted to know the interior image, the hidden meanings.

After class Strand asked Nelson, "So what do you make of her?"

He raised his eyebrows, his fleshy face creased with a wide smile. In their years of friendship Strand had never revealed curiosity about anyone. Except him. Her other personal relationships were brief, ephemeral, significant only when they were discarded, material to dissect over dinner and wine.

"Girlfriend, I know what you know. She's mother nature's creature, but not one I've ever seen before."

"Empath."

"I got the silver hair thing," Nelson answered impatiently. "But she never moves. Shit's racing around inside there, though. You know?"

"Um."

"I've seen her a couple of times at Ruby's, always with the hat though."

"Why would she go to that greasy spoon?"

"Why would *I* go? To eat some greens, to look at folks, and to keep the Joneses from keeping up with you."

"Ruby's?"

"Yeah." Nelson worked hard to sound as noncommittal as Strand.

"See you tomorrow," Strand said, walking away, not sure herself what thoughts she hid.

"Earth to Strand," Nelson said when he realized Strand had fallen asleep on the table. "Where do you go in there? You were out for the count."

She sat up quickly, startled. "Let's go light on the tranq next time, whew!"

"Sometimes I wish I could hook up some speakers to that brain of yours."

"What? So you can fall asleep too!" Strand laughed as he helped her down from the table.

He sprayed a thin layer of surgical fixative, then handed Strand, ever distrustful of Dupont, one of the oversized T-shirts she now wore beneath all of her clothes. He watched her drape it as gently as he did his easel. He avoided touching her back as they embraced, smiling at the soft texture of her hair on the side of his cheek.

"Tomorrow and tomorrow and tomorrow. Isn't that some movie?" The sparkle in Strand's eyes concealed whether she thought she was joking or not. Nelson held the intercom open so she could hear him still laughing down in the lobby and out into the courtyard.

Back in her own flat, she sipped a tall glass of water, hoping to hurry the tranquilizer from her system. She never slept until Lynx rang the phone once to signal she was home. If she let it ring more than once they'd talk. Strand laid across the bed; when the phone rang for the third time she pressed the button in the bed's headboard.

"Hello, I hope it's not too late." Lynx's voice still carried the softness of the middle of the country.

"Hi, I just got home from Nelson's."

"Did you two have a good time?"

A ray of amusement glinted through the awkward necessity of sounding casual. The Joneses randomly listened to telephone conversations in the housing complex.

"Great," Strand answered. "He's a wonderful artist." Her belief in the praise was undisguised.

"Have you eaten?" Lynx asked.

"I'm too beat."

"I'll let you go then. I just wanted to...to get in touch."

"Thanks, let's get together soon." Strand became impatient with the form they followed so cautiously.

"Wonderful. I was hoping you'd be open." A smile suffused Lynx's voice.

"What about tomorrow?"

"Perfect, I have a new piece I'd like to show you." Lynx barely suppressed laughter.

Strand clicked off and laid back down. In the last year and a half she and Lynx had kept their relationship quiet, rarely going out as a couple. Only when they were together in one of their flats did they allow their need for each other to spill out in words and touch. For months it had been like a game they played: tricking the Joneses. Now it was a tight band around Strand's chest squeezing her breath, smothering her. But Lynx's attempts at erotic humor made her smile. She sounded weary, Strand thought, as she plummeted into sleep.

SESSION #82

"What?" Strand said without looking away from her monitor. She'd shifted light and color on the brand-new sedan for the past hour and nothing made it appealing, unusual, or seem like a necessity. When Freda didn't answer, Strand looked away from the screen in frustration. "What is it?"

Freda, secretary on Strand's floor for almost five years, stood tentatively in the doorway. The intelligence in her eyes was sometimes shadowed by the stress of working in advertising, but more often by her inability to comprehend Strand. Freda's mind and her short, round body moved with equal dexterity around the political pot-holes of Broadcast One, and she knew she was one of the reasons Strand had a successful career. But it was never clear how Strand felt about this.

"I talked to Dee, in the pool. She's got those contracts covered. I'm going—"

"What about Dee?" Strand said, still unable to focus on her secretary.

"She's going to finish those contracts you just gave me. Remember, I have my videography class tonight."

"Dee can't do this, Freda. I need you on this one. We're using too many specialists on this shoot, everyone has a contract. I've got to have it first thing in the morning—done right."

"Dee's good, Strand. I've got her set up, and I'll log in and check her work after my class."

"Then what? If she fucks up I'm screwed."

"If there are mistakes I'll have time—"

"Freda, do you work for me or not?" Strand turned back to the monitor, stared at the wash of red, and began to calibrate its intensity. "I'm leaving here at 7:00."

Freda bit back a reply and tried to keep in mind the exhilaration she felt when the two of them talked about a successful video shoot. She quietly shut the door to Strand's office and returned to her desk.

When Strand swung through the pool to leave at 7:15, Freda raised the stack of contracts with a trim smile.

"I always tell them you're the best, Freda!" Strand said as she pressed the elevator button.

At Nelson's house Strand stepped out of her clothes with the same ease as she'd forgotten the exchange with Freda. Nelson inspected his mix of colors and the needle machine. Strand laid her pants and tunic neatly on the back of an overstuffed reading chair Nelson had rescued from a theater where he'd designed a set. Gazing into an ornate mirror over the couch, she thought she looked fuller without her clothes. The slowing metabolism of her middle years was revealed in her hips and thighs. Tonight the thickening made her smile.

"Any ripples outside?" Nelson asked.

"No." Strand tried to dismiss the increasing unease she'd felt over the past few weeks.

"I'm just gonna go back to do a few lines. I don't want to work too long."

"Up or down?" she asked.

"Down."

Strand stretched out on her stomach with a sigh.

"Sometimes the work just comes, like squeezed out of a tube. Other times I can't hook in. Does that make sense?"

"It's taking longer than you thought."

Nelson turned his attention to the line on Strand's thigh.

"We'll all get together soon.

"Good idea."

"Remember that first time?"

"Uh-huh."

"I'll never be that way again, will I, Nelson?"

He raised the machine. "No, I don't think so."

Then he was immersed in the work, his breathing in tune with the machine and its vibrating needles. Strand strained upward to look at the natural lines he drew on her thighs, the ink perfectly distributed, blood welling around it. She closed her eyes and tried to remember the moment the change had begun.

The entire class worked intently at their easels. Strand avoided meeting Nelson's eyes for a smile as they occasionally did. Just before the session ended, she pushed her easel to the edge of the studio, then slipped out.

On the street, instinct took over as it did when she worked. Pictures were what guided her. The image of Ruby's drew her: a narrow, brick structure on the edge of the city, with a brightly lit window where they served messy food to people who stayed far into the night.

She'd had dinner there once with Nelson and some of his friends, all the while unnerved by the noise and aimlessly circular discussions. She imagined the entire place to be under the shadow of a brown cloud, the effluvia of frying foods and overlong bantering.

Watching through a window of the rumbling jitney, she recognized the long, light-filled window as they passed, but stayed on

Did he purposely leave out age until now?

just the beginning how dear woman

board for several more blocks to get a clearer sense of the neighborhood. She leapt out in front of the darkened facade of a beauty salon and made her way back to Ruby's entrance. She stood between the double set of glass doors beside a public telephone. At first she saw only her own reflection: tall, unyielding posture accentuated by the spare lines of her fullsuit which hugged the curves of her body. Her skin, the shade of golden oak, was unlined at the age of forty. The tight row of braids curving around the crown of her head was accurately austere, threaded with gray. She appreciated the image without smiling.

Behind her the sound of laughter and shouted food orders floated through the cafe. She shifted her gaze, looking out through the glass more intently than she'd ever looked at anything other than a studio set. She wondered what she'd do if Lynx didn't recognize her.

The muted green of the crocheted cap alerted Strand as Lynx came down the street toward the cafe. Strand pulled the door open just as Lynx stood before it. She brushed hesitancy aside and said "Surprise" in the lightest voice she could muster. The cloud lifted from the ice of Lynx's eyes, which lightened almost to amber as she laughed. She tried to say Strand's name but couldn't stop laughing. Strand attempted to offer her a drink; Lynx's laughter was, however, uncontrollable. The hidden catch broken, mirth enveloped Lynx so totally it was alarming. Lynx grabbed Strand's arm as if to stop herself from falling.

"Let me hold on, please, just a moment. Please," she said between eruptions. Strand watched steadily, not understanding what it meant, regretting she'd followed her impulse. Lynx's grip began to bruise her arm. The color in Lynx's eyes darkened as she felt Strand's pain, and the laughter stopped. She let go of Strand, wiping tears from the corners of her eyes.

"I just wanted..." The words strangled each other in Strand's throat. "I startled you."

Lynx smiled. "It happens so rarely. I'm sorry I frightened you."

"You didn't."

"Yes, I did. And I am sorry. I'll never become used to living among people." Lynx's voice was only partly playful.

"Yeah, I know what you mean."

"Yes, you do." Lynx's eyes narrowed as she peered at Strand. "You're the one in the figure class."

"Strand."

"Yes." The sibilants slipped from Lynx's mouth like taffy. Slow, intriguing.

"I was just leaving."

"Oh?" Lynx was puzzled at the lie she could feel all around them. Noise filled Strand's ears, blocking out Lynx's voice. She took a deep breath and caught the soft scent of soap. "Excuse me," Strand said cooly, then stepped around Lynx and escaped through the doors.

Strand shifted on the table, thinking about that first time. How alien her discomfort with Lynx felt now.

"Okay, girlfriend, that's it for tonight." Nelson's voice broke into her thoughts. "I got the right perspective. Finally! It's going to be perfect."

He sprayed ceremoniously.

"Don't look, come on now, don't look. You can't see anything anyhow!"

Uncharacteristically obedient, Strand didn't try to examine the work. Instead she turned sideways in the ornate mirror and admired the small tattoo of an old-fashioned bicycle on her calf—a large spoked wheel with a much smaller one behind.

"What'd you call this again?"

"A pennyfarthing." Nelson had done it in the first year of their friendship, saying, "It'll take you anywhere you want to go." He started cleaning up his instruments. "If anybody asks we were sketching..." He trailed off, waiting.

"Kitchen utensils and Warhol." Strand provided their alibi with a laugh.

"Ugh!" Nelson shuddered. "Don't be letting nobody be patting you."

"Yes, I know, I know."

At the end of every session the project seemed riskier than the day before. The Society didn't care for the renegade art of tattooing anymore than it did for travel to the West. Legislation had banned the art in the nineteenth century. Now, two hundred years later, the laws had been reenacted. Nelson felt like the proprietor of one of the needle parlors he'd read about in his historical novels, in which squalid back rooms catering to drunken sailors dotted the water-front.

Strand left Nelson's studio a little dazed as the drug wore off and the pain of the needles reached her. It'd been more than a year since she and Lynx had become lovers, something else the Society would frown on. She hurried toward Lynx's room, a tiny garret space looking out over a factory loading dock. She let herself in and rubbed Lynx's cat and dog in response to their eager greetings, wondering how they decided who to like and who to snub. Few people kept pets in the Society, so it still felt a little strange to have small, living things moving around her.

Strand lay on her stomach across the bed where the cat and dog circled after they finished eating. She didn't move at the sound of Lynx's step on the stairs, only listened, feeling her body come alive with the waiting. *Sexual undertone*

Lynx hummed as she entered her room, lowered herself to the bed, and cautiously pulled the shirt over Strand's head. The waves of her hair were tied back in a white ribbon. Her uniform was rumpled and stained with hours of sweat. She kissed one of the parts in Strand's hair and, without speaking, massaged Strand's head, running her strong fingers along the rows of braids. They were a pale shade of blue this week, dyed to match an outfit she'd worn for a film premiere. Strand and Nelson had made a striking pair in twin outfits: high visibility meant more jobs. Tired of finding scarves to match, Strand swore that before the weekend her hair would be its usual silver-flecked brown again.

Lynx worked her way down Strand's neck and shoulders, massaging the muscles gently. Soon Strand felt the heat of Lynx's hands as they passed above the raw skin where Nelson had been working. Lynx held her palms just over the solid lines and the wash of bronze and silver that he'd created on Strand's back. Lynx's breath quickened, and she resisted drawing away the wound completely—taking in all the pain risked the durability of the picture. She drew out a portion of the burning, pulling it into herself and releasing it into the air. She worked quickly, anxious to be done with the healing and to feel Strand's body more intimately. *similar to "The giver"*

The lines that lay across and down Strand's back were intriguingly familiar to Lynx. Even unfinished, they began to take shape and open themselves to her. She held her hand steady and continued to trace the outline of pale color, making Strand's skin first warm then cool.

As Lynx worked, Strand wondered how they'd feel when the tattoo was done, and a shiver of fear rippled across her skin.

"How did it go today?"

"Nelson's pleased. He says I have good legs. Soon they'll be twice as good." Strand smiled, but Lynx did not.

"Earlier, when I was at the hospital, I was resting between patients and I closed my eyes. I saw blood. Spilling down your flesh."

"At the beginning I tried to watch Nelson working."

"Tried?"

"I didn't watch long. Not like me, being squeamish, is it?"

"Not like you at all, Strand."

"Do you want us to stop?"

"It's a bit like dying. I've felt that with patients, you know. A loosening inside myself."

"Should we stop?"

"No."

The muscles in Strand's body relaxed. The heat now emanating from her body was not from the wounds. Lynx touched the inside of Strand's thigh lightly, then entered her from behind.

SESSION #90

While they waited for the sedative to take effect, Nelson showed Strand one of his old books, its pages wrinkled and soft. The pictures from the early 1900s depicted men and women with primitive tattoos covering most of their bodies: flowery hearts, battleships, flags. Other pages reproduced the more sophisticated tattoos of indigenous people from some of the Pacific Islands. The tight lines and bands were so compelling, Strand knew the project was the right thing to do. She began disrobing, looking at the bric-a-brac crowding Nelson's shelves.

"What's this little car?"

"Isn't it great. See those wheels? Whitewall tires, fabulous!" Nelson plucked the replica of the antique Stutz Bearcat from his bookshelf. Its trim design felt solid in his hand. "This was a real car. My grandfather used to say he knew western civilization was doomed when all the cars started looking alike. Alfa Romeo, Mercedes, Cadillac, Jag, Saab, Mustang—by the turn of the century the designs were interchangeable."

"He could have been right," Strand said. The pleasure Nelson took in his memories of his family pleased her, even though she had none of her own. Each session was an interior journey for them both. They exchanged history and ideas with an urgency and intimacy few citizens bothered with in Society City. At the same time that Strand listened to Nelson's stories, or told her own, she was traveling away from everything she knew about herself to a destination she couldn't yet picture in her mind.

[margin note: remark on society although acceptab only superfica.]

She climbed onto the table, relinquishing her body to Nelson's hand. The light markings he made as a guide tickled her skin.

"I'm going back to the right shoulder today. Warn me if you need to stop. But no fidgeting."

"I'll be fine."

"Yeah, I know you're tough. But don't wait 'til you're ready to leap from the table before you say uncle, okay?"

Strand slipped easily under the spell of the needle's high-pitched hum. The first touch was like a small bite, then the sensation radiated out in dull waves of stimulation. Nelson told her that traditional tattoo artists hadn't used tranquilizers. She didn't see why he insisted she take them, yet the vivid memories they induced usually pleased her.

On the final day of the figure-drawing cycle, the end of Lynx's work as their model, Nelson cajoled Strand into having a drink with him at Ruby's Cafe. He returned waves and shouts from other customers as they took a table by the windows. Within minutes of ordering drinks, Nelson leapt from his seat and dashed to the front where Lynx stood hesitantly inside the glass double doors. She smiled when she saw Nelson. Strand felt annoyed and trapped as Nelson and Lynx headed back to the table.

After eight weeks of art class, Nelson and Strand were the only two willing to acknowledge Lynx; everyone else fled as if she would read their minds for sport. Strand had never managed more than a studied *hello* each session, following her first misstep, but that was more than the rest of the workshop participants. The din of Ruby's swirled around them for the next half hour while they endured stilted attempts at conversation: about the drawing they'd seen in the studio class, about professional development, about the neighborhood.

Ruby, the owner, was behind the bar—six feet tall and sloe-eyed, commanding the room even when she was just washing the glasses. She brought a bottle of wine and refilled their glasses without being called, greeting Nelson familiarly.

"You're not switching on me, are ya?" she asked, smiling at Lynx and Strand.

Nelson gay?

"Not yet. Lynx, Strand, this is the inestimable Ruby."

"He promised I'm first if he gets the urge."

"And who was it that was gonna protect me from Danny?"

"When I finished with you, sweetie, you'd need hospital rest anyway." Ruby's laughter filled the restaurant as she went back to the bar.

Strand watched, puzzled. She hadn't realized Nelson was such a regular at Ruby's. When they ate dinner out it was usually in their own part of town, near the complex. As Ruby's laughter trailed off, Lynx spoke. "Will you tell me about tattoos?"

Nelson hesitated only a moment before breaking into the smile that Strand recognized as his preface to a story. Strand was surprised again, this time at his open enthusiasm: neither of them were sure precisely where empaths stood in the Joneses' family tree.

"It's fine to talk with me," Lynx answered the unspoken question and lightly rested her freckled hand on Strand's arm. A comforting sensation pulsed through Lynx's fingers to Strand. Nelson began to tell her some of the history of body adornment, about his books, the lore.

"They all tattooed something they thought they needed. Even when it was just boasting, it was still wishful thinking. I saw yearning, urgency, in the tiniest rose resting on someone's hip bone; it was like nothing in the galleries.

"I was looking for the images that filled me up, not just paint on paper. When I did my first tattoo I knew I had it." He watched closely for Lynx's reaction before he went on.

"The purr of the electricity is exciting. When the needles prick flesh I almost feel it. The entering, the connecting, are exhilarating. And then there's the picture, eternal in a mortal kind of way."

"I don't know if I could bear the intrusion," Lynx said.

"It's not for everybody. You've got to understand the meaning of taking on an image, of taking that image inside yourself. Once you do, you can stand anything, I think."

Lynx smiled at Nelson, and Strand watched her intently.

"Hey, I don't want you two to think this is a setup, but I'm out of here." Nelson fumbled under the table for his case, at the same time looking toward the door.

"What?" Strand said, her annoyance escalating to anger.

"Sorry, I've got a late date."

Strand stared coldly at him, then at the smiling man standing in the doorway.

"Don't give me that look, girlfriend. Be sociable, I'm going to be." Nelson pulled his long, full sweater from the back of the chair.

"See ya, right?" he smiled at Lynx.

"I hope so."

"My treat." He waved at them in the mirror and paid Ruby at the bar before sweeping out the door.

"I apologize. Nelson doesn't usually make a fool of himself in front of people, especially over men."

"No need. I hoped we'd get the chance to talk."

Strand thought about the tone and shape of Lynx's voice. The elongated vowels made it seem as if she were speaking with great deliberation, thinking in another language. Lynx sat almost as still as she did in class, waiting. They sipped the rest of their drinks in silence.

"What was it like growing up...being an empath?" Strand finally asked, reaching for her training in social manners. The shadow which crossed Lynx's face made Strand regret her inquiry. Lynx spoke quickly, her voice low and hoarse.

"My mother, Mae, figured I was weak. Melancholy too, I guess. She's a plain woman. Not much for cities or books. She must have thought that empaths were creatures the Society made up, like hobgoblins. Frankensteins they cooked up in labs or something." Lynx laughed.

"As I got older Mae just thought I was mad. And I was, for a while."

Lynx looked around the room as if others might have heard her last words. But the music from the old stereo speakers still washed over the rise and fall of conversation, the clink of dishes and glassware. The noise shielded Lynx from them, but it could not protect her. The exultation of a woman and man—bathed in desire, sitting impatiently at a back table—radiated across the room. The cold fury of a young woman sitting at the counter pierced Lynx's skin. Their waiter's exhaustion, as he set down their drinks, sapped her strength.

"I can feel all of it, the deepest things they feel. Him, her, them," she said, nodding her head around the room. "Swirling inside me. Back then I thought I was possessed. I couldn't escape, and I couldn't explain what was happening."

"Children from the farms nearby made fun of me when they saw me sitting with our cows in the pasture instead of going to school. Their parents pointed at me and followed me around whenever I went to town. Mae tried...why do people think experiencing curiosity automatically gives them the right to your life?" The urgency in Lynx's voice made Strand want to touch her. Lynx took a breath and went on.

"Then my hair began to change. The silver ate through the red and for the first time I really loved something about myself. I didn't care who stared. Mae used to brush it every night for the longest time. But I could feel her fear. Then they came and took me away."

The words alarmed Strand, who'd never paid much attention to who empaths were, where they'd come from, or how they served Society. In that moment, she felt a part of the "they" who'd come to take Lynx from her home. One of the Joneses.

"I was tranquilized for a year. Therapists did exercises with my body, they fed me intravenously most of that time. Control voices were played almost constantly on implants." Lynx lifted her unusual hair away from her neck and displayed the tiny line where the incision had been made. Strand, with years of practice, easily concealed any obvious reaction.

"It was like living outside my body, a twelve-month dream. And when they thought I'd be able to protect myself from the tumult of feeling, they took me off the tranqs and started to train me."

"What do you mean 'train'?"

"Most empaths acquire the sensitivity later in life, after we've already learned how to preserve individuality. I was too young and susceptible to everyone. I had to be trained to open and close, to draw in and release the sensations without being subsumed by them."

"The Society doesn't give anything away for free." Strand's suspicions rose.

"Society's correctional hospitals, the health care system, they couldn't function without us. We're their intellectual property, in a manner of speaking."

Pride was new to Lynx. She'd experienced it for the first time when she was able to move inside the pain of another and help untangle it. She maintained a precarious balance between that joy and a sense of being used for purposes she could not know.

"But we have to be supervised so our health doesn't wear down. I fought to be allowed to live in the city, to work with children, not just with convicted offenders."

"Why here?"

"The training tapes hadn't really worked. I thought I could train myself to be around people in one of the cities. But now I'm either completely closed down, like when I'm modeling for the class, or too open, like when I think of you."

Strand looked from Lynx to her glass, keeping her noncommittal expression in place.

"I feel you so much and I want to know you," Lynx said, a crimson flush rising from her neck to her cheeks.

Strand didn't speak but took a sip from her glass.

"I know what you're feeling too. I'm sorry, I can't help it. I know."

"How can you?" Strand said, her voice wavering only slightly. To be known frightened her more than she'd ever admitted to herself.

"I've been trying to explain. I more than know, I feel what you're feeling. You can't hide from me even when you run away like you did that first time. I watched you through the window as you left. I felt the battle inside you."

Strand leaned back from the table as if to leave.

"Don't—" Lynx gripped Strand, pressing her hand into the rough wood edge of the tiny table. "Push away! That was your feeling just then. But you want to sink inside me, too. It's all there coursing through your body. Your facility to keep it bricked up inside is amazing."

Strand looked down at their hands locked together, expecting them to glow with the heat she felt.

"You look at my fingers and want them in your mouth," Lynx said with an edge of wonder. "You want my fingers pressing inside your mouth, you sucking, pulling, tasting."

Strand glared at their hands. Her gaze did not soften as she looked up into Lynx's eyes.

"Why does desire make you want to hurt me? Or is it the knowing? Do you want to marry your fear?" Lynx asked. She inhaled so deeply it felt impossibly long, then removed her hand.

Strand felt the weight of abandonment at the release of Lynx's hand as she'd never experienced it before. Even on the worst days living in the Society orphanage. Then her breath caught in her chest as if Lynx had been holding her hand over her mouth and nose, stopping the air. She gasped and breathed deeply, her chest heaving.

"I'm going to have to give you another tranq, Strand." Nelson stretched his arms above his head. "You're acting up."

"What?" Strand said, disoriented.

"You're starting to thrash around."

She opened her eyes and saw, spread out under her shoulder, the towel spotted with her blood.

"Oh."

"Take this," Nelson said, thrusting the glass of green liquid toward her. The bent plastic straw reached in her direction.

"I'm fine, just a dream."

Nelson's hand was steady; the glass did not retreat.

Strand yielded, ran her tongue over the straw, then drew a small amount of the liquid in. She closed her eyes to await the relaxation.

"You've got to be still as stone here, girl. I want not a hair out of place."

"I'm sorry. I drift away, into the past."

"How about talking to me. About anything, as long as you stay still."

Many times she and Nelson had sat together, in bars, parks, telling each other their life stories, being each other's confidant in a way that was more common to adolescents than adults. They'd both come to the capital from small towns in the north, near New Hampshire's border, where the highway leading to Society City was the yellow brick road for anyone who wanted to be an artist. They each had done work that had caught the attention of local councilors early in their careers, and had each petitioned and won the opportunity to move to the City.

They'd spied each other one day in the Art Park at the center of the housing compound where they lived. Dwelling on opposite ends of a complex of high-rises built explicitly for art workers, neither often crossed the expanse of regimentally manicured green lawn adorning its center. The Park resembled a miniature baseball diamond, but instead of bases there were strategically placed pieces of art meant to inspire the residents, some of whom sat sketching or writing in their shadows.

Despite Strand's disdain for the programmed nature of their artistic environment, she'd requested permission to remain in the artists' compound after she began working in advertising and broadcast. One visit to the complexes designed for media professionals, and Strand had known they were too shiny and noisy for her. Painting was quiet, and the click of computer keys was less to contend with than the endless static of broadcast voices emptied of their regional shadings. She much preferred the trite Modigliani imitations and Romare Beardon rip-offs to the premieres and festivals that sprawled across the huge screens dominating the media complexes.

The Society liked imitation; perfect replication was as prized as any original. She and Nelson smirked in secret about the imitative nature of the artwork around them. No matter how crowded and tough the City was, neither of them wanted to be sent to some outpost like Chicago to design stamps or traffic signs.

A new Richard Serra replica resembling a rusted flying wedge was installed in the outfield soon after they'd met. Strand came upon Nelson late one night tossing a pair of shoes, tied together by their laces, into the air, trying to land them across the fourteen-foot-high slab of metal. His drunken state was making his aim unpredictable, so Strand grabbed the shoes and tossed expertly, leaving the muddy size twelves dangling irreverently. *↳ typical dyke*

"City kids, poor ones, used to do that all over the country years ago," he said, laughing.

"Why would poor people throw away their shoes?" she asked, genuinely perplexed.

"Who knows? To leave their mark, to keep being poor from running their lives?" He shrugged.

Strand pushed herself to imagine that time before the Society corporatized, when children would be allowed to throw away shoes. "Maybe they just wanted to see how high they could throw," she speculated.

They'd been friends ever since.

"Well?" Nelson said, putting down the electric needles he used to insert bright colors under her skin. He rinsed and dried his hands, then took up a sketching crayon.

"Tell me how Lynx is doing," he said.

Strand always felt his inquiries about Lynx were as much about herself as Lynx. "She's having a difficult time controlling the barrage of sensations. She takes the blocking drugs when she has to, but they slow her work and numb her for anything else."

"What about that hypnotist I told you about?"

"She ended up hypnotizing him."

Nelson would have laughed had he not heard the strain in Strand's voice.

"When she comes home she lies in the dark, sometimes for hours, like a corpse, trying to recover."

"The Joneses aren't going to let their valuable property go on like that for long."

"The more she opens to me, the less strength she has to screen out everyone else. Her supervisor is already insisting she go on blockers all the time. She'll end up immobilized in a hospital with medicos bringing patients to her bedside for healing like she's some kind of ghoul."

"Steady."

Strand concentrated on lying still, then said, "I want to watch you in the mirror."

"Come on, you don't want to do that."

He felt her body stiffen and knew her well enough to recognize her on the edge of fury. He pulled over a small table and placed his shaving mirror and another small hand mirror at angles so that she could watch him work.

"I'm going back to the leg lines."

Strand observed the arch of Nelson's wrist and felt the soft tip of the pencil on her calves. The grip of his fingers was echoed in the determined set of his lips. It was a look she'd seen often in their art class and on the dance floor.

"You talk."

A shiver went through her when he picked up the needle. Such a barbaric custom, she thought. Funny how it had lasted so long despite attempts to outlaw it. Almost everyone had a tattoo or two or three created by the quick and relatively painless laser implements. They were designed to wear off in several months.

Strand felt the muted sting of the needle on the back of her leg and watched the blood rise in the track behind the needle. The line extending up her calf to her thigh was fascinating to her, as if she were reading her palm. Nelson worked with steady deliberation, his eyes never leaving the line. She couldn't see the color of the dye, only the dark red which sometimes welled up and slipped down the side of her leg. She felt curiously ill for a moment and sniffed in surprise.

"You all right?"

"I was just thinking—"

"Please, no thinking. Talk."

"I'm not certain how you expect me to do the latter without the former."

"Chatter is good for the soul."

Strand closed her eyes. "We finally got permission for our trip to the country, for a week. Soon."

She waited for Nelson to get to the end of a line and lift his head.

"It's not my favorite thing to do in the middle of a piece, but I guess it's time."

"Her mother still feels guilty letting them take her."

"What's to feel guilty about? When the Joneses want to take you away, that's what they do. Mother or no mother." His voice deepened with emotion.

"Maybe when she sees us together she'll know it's for the best. And Lynx can see the farm animals she loves."

Strand was quiet as Nelson set to work again. Strand knew that growing up with livestock had made it easy for Lynx to have pets when she moved to the city. She also understood why most people living in cities disapproved of keeping pets, although from the beginning Nelson had never said anything negative about it. And after she'd seen Lynx with them—the thin, dark dog called Sliver and the fat black-and-white fur ball of a cat called Dot, both scampering in to be with Lynx when she needed them—Strand had accepted it. She was even looking forward to encountering a live cow.

"Quiet for a minute while I get this last bit." She could feel Nelson thinking.

"All right," he said after a few moments of work. "That's it for the time being. I'd let that heal some on its own before I'd do a lot of sitting."

Strand laughed at the maternal timbre of his voice and slipped into her oversized shirt and loose pants. She missed the one-piece simplicity of her fullsuit, but was beginning to enjoy the sensation of the soft folds of fabric brushing her skin as she moved.

By the time she was back in her own high-rise apartment the dulling effect of the tranq was beginning to thin and Strand was hungry. She ignored the beep of her mailbox and started dinner. Lynx was on duty at the correctional hospital and wouldn't call until later. Strand wanted to have eaten and gotten comfortable by then; this was a night they'd get to talk. Looking at the perfectly balanced picture her dinner plate made, she laughed at her own obsession with visual presentation, then deliberately sloshed the food around.

Strand stood in front of the mail screen with her food and clicked on her messages as she began to eat. The word OVERRIDE filled the square of light, then the message:

> TO: <smb@art.pro.res> Ms. Strand Maria Burroughs
> Your presence is required tomorrow at 9 am in the office
> of the Deputy Director of Social Security. This office is
> located on the 4th floor of the Society City Bureau on
> Broadway and Main Street. Please be prompt. Expect to
> remain for a period of 2 hours. Areas of discussion: Art-
> ists' Compound, Constructive social contacts. Your em-
> ployer, Broadcast One, has been informed of this required
> absence.

Strand hit the print button just to be certain it was as she'd read it
on the screen. As the printer spooled and reproduced the message,
she dumped her food in the disposal and filled a glass with white
wine. She read the message again, the paper trembling in her hand.

Her living room was not especially large, but its picture window
faced the city skyline and made it feel cavernous at night. Strand
paced in front of the backdrop of twinkling lights, oblivious to all
except the piece of paper in her hand. She peered at the places where
she knew the computer program had dropped the particulars of the
message into the form: her name, her employer's name, time, areas
of discussion. *Constructive social contacts.* That could mean anything.
But they'd said Artists' Compound. It must be something about her
and Nelson.

The phone rang.

"Yes?"

"What is it?" Lynx said after a breath of hesitation.

"I'll meet you at the mirrors when you're done."

"Now." Lynx broke the connection immediately.

Strand hurriedly typed a message to Nelson: "I hope you found
the note I left. See you tomorrow. SMB." Strand had been almost
certain they'd never have to use this prearranged warning and as she
hit SEND the message seemed both ominous and silly.

It was logical that someone would find out about the tattoo even-
tually; questions would be raised. The Society was benevolent, but
only to a point. The intersection of kind concern and control was
located wherever any event occurred which the Joneses didn't understand, or which could be construed as disruptive.

Strand hoped Nelson wouldn't be out all night or forget to check his messages in time to hide his treasured machines. Along with architectural miniatures and toy cars, over the years he'd obtained a collection of antique tattoo irons. If the DSS decided to sweep through, tattoo needles would spark more attention than replicas of old tourist sites.

She slammed out the door and waited impatiently for the elevator, trying not to let anxiety swallow her. One of Society City's ubiquitous jitneys pulled up faster than the elevator had and she stood in front of the mirrored bar at Ruby's before Lynx arrived. The place was eerie at such a late hour, almost lifeless without the noise of a full bar. Ruby greeted her with a smile and poured a glass of the wine she usually drank.

Strand tried not to gulp as she watched through the glass doors. She felt dread as she had the first evening, but this time when she saw Lynx push the double doors open escape was not on her mind. Lynx approached warily, unused to seeing Strand off balance. She read the letter in a glance.

"I don't know what it means," Strand said, her voice almost steady, "but people down at the Department of Social Security are more about security than social. Assume they know about the tattoo." Her tension was a hard wind against Lynx's skin.

"We have to make the trip to my mother." There was no plea in Lynx's voice.

"I know. They're probably watching us."

"They always watch empaths."

Strand stared through the window and realized she was almost never out this late. "Sometimes I hate this city. Even being outside is like being inside. Under a roof with everyone spying."

Lynx wanted to reassure Strand but was unsure how to go about it. Stating the facts was what Strand seemed to need right now. "Every day they get closer to demanding what they really want. I've been trained to slip inside of others, to manipulate what they feel or know in order to heal them. But not everyone can be healed." Lynx's voice was barely a whisper. Strand leaned closer but resisted her desire to touch her arm.

"I've done things for the Society I can't think about at night. I won't go on, Strand."

"We're almost done." Strand dug deeply for her confidence, but uncertainty clouded her words. "Maybe the three of us should go to your mother's and finish."

"We stay relaxed, listening. Not exuding."

"What?" Strand leaned on the bar, imagining herself with water spouting from her head or stuffing leaking from her seams.

"It's almost like that," Lynx laughed, reading the picture. "What you feel rolls off of you like waves. Even when you're perfectly still. Remember that tomorrow. If this is serious, they're sure to have an empath there to listen."

"I handle bureaucrats every day at Broadcast."

"Everything is different now, Strand. Don't concentrate on blocking your feelings like you usually do. Focus on taking in what they're exuding."

The expression on Strand's face didn't change. Lynx could feel her doubt.

"You can do it. Take the concentration you usually use to close yourself off. Reverse it. Don't worry about what they can get from you, listen to them. Listen hard."

Strand felt exposed in the glare of Ruby's lights and glass.

"We better get going," she said. "We'll still do the trip."

Lynx nodded, the tight braid of her bright curls hanging heavily down her back. Strand put her arm around her shoulder as they walked outside, glancing nervously up the street. Once Lynx had boarded a jitney, Strand watched to see if anyone emerged and followed. City lights and pollution made it impossible to see stars. The night was bright and empty.

Strand let go of her thoughts and tried to float free, listening to what was in the air. A wall of night sound blurred around her, its almost indecipherable noises buffeting her. She focused outward and let the night speak. The noise rose to a din. Behind her she heard the soft murmur of thoughts and voices from a window above. She relaxed into listening and could distinguish the sounds of individuals—a child, two men, a woman alone—floating around her head like cumulus clouds. She began to understand what Lynx lived with every day.

Then Ruby pulled the front door shut behind her with an end-of-day finality and Strand remembered where she was. She hurried home to decide what to wear to her meeting.

The next morning Strand opened the door to the fourth floor office of the Department of Social Security at exactly 9:00 A.M. The clean lines of the office had been amplified to austerity: prim chrome chairs, blank walls, no magazines. The receptionist blossomed with good cheer despite the hour and her surroundings.

The Department of Social Security, the largest of the government's privately run agencies, kept track of all the citizens and their financial status, making certain they paid taxes and traffic tickets. It monitored who studied what disciplines to be certain the market wasn't glutted; who married whom to keep pace with population growth; and who lived where, to be certain neighborhoods were developed symmetrically. All was accomplished with a congenial smile and decrees that had no court of appeal. Citizens felt secure, and most had easily forgotten privacy. Freedom came through careful management of the population, including early elimination of potential trouble spots.

Strand was feeling like one of those spots when two people in gray suits looked up at her as the receptionist showed her into the office.

"Ms. Burroughs, thank you for joining us," said the man. "I'm Dr. Skinner and this is Professor McKinnon."

"How do you do, Doctor. Professor," Strand replied in her best orphanage-trained voice. She recognized the professor as an author of some of the theories in which the Society was grounded. Strand knew McKinnon had written somewhere that the population needed to be protected from itself, from its baser instincts. Women, in McKinnon's mind, were especially vulnerable.

Strand watched their bodies. They were curiously alike despite the gender difference—tight, angular—each suspended in a carefully constructed air of nonchalance. Then she listened. Not especially to what they asked her, but to what they didn't ask and to what they thought of her answers.

"We realize it's early, can we bring you tea or coffee?" Professor McKinnon asked congenially. Strand noticed the perfection of her

[handwritten in left margin: 1984]

[handwritten at bottom: Best story so for— Doesn't blatantly push the subject]

teeth and how uninflected her voice was, as if she were a television anchor rather than a bureaucrat.

"Yes, thank you." The office door opened and the receptionist stuck her head in.

"I was thinking of making some tea. Would you like a pot in here, Doctor?"

"Yes, thank you." Dr. Skinner seemed burdened by the necessity to appear pleasant. Strand could feel him restraining himself, capping his surliness. She assumed the questions would be pro forma until the receptionist returned with the tea and departed. But they began immediately, asking about her relationship with Nelson. They hinted at speculation about the intimacy of the friendship. If they had been courting, the DSS was interested in how long before marriage might be expected, what the combined incomes and buying power would be.

"We're both queer!" Strand was puzzled they didn't know something as public as that. The Society no longer penalized homosexual citizens, but monitored them subtly to satisfy conservative fears and to predict economic trends.

"Yes, of course, but that hasn't precluded bonding in some cases."

Strand listened to the swing of their words in the air. Bonding occurred between all kinds of people for a variety of reasons, but the Society expected formally posted bans before any commingling of households took place so that census and tax records could be maintained.

The receptionist slipped in quietly as they continued talking and set the teapot on a side table. As Strand watched the shape of their bodies and the auras surrounding each of them, she realized that she could hear the receptionist listening to her. It was just as Lynx had said, an empath—the receptionist—was taking everything in.

Strand stayed open, observing, not thinking. She could feel the receptionist's continued attention just outside the door while she answered most of the inquiries by rote.

"Have you considered that there might be more than friendship between you? At least on one side?"

Strand felt deep surprise as she registered the question.

"No," she said hesitantly. "No, I really haven't. We spend time

Examination by the society

together, but..." Her voice trailed off as she watched them seem to gather themselves, becoming taller, more authoritative.

"We noticed you both declared in the same religion on your tax returns." McKinnon's smile had too many sides.

Strand shrugged with amusement. You had to fill in a box so she'd filled in a box. She knew Nelson felt the same.

"We don't want to push anything, my dear," Skinner said. "But think about it. If he's bisexual, you must take things into consideration. What signals you're giving—"

"Misunderstanding and miscommunication lead us to mistakes and misgivings," McKinnon broke in. Strand recognized her quoting from her own writing.

She almost expected them to ask, "What are your intentions toward our daughter?" Instead they smiled at her as if they shared a secret. She returned their gaze diffusely. Her back felt irritated so she shifted forward in her chair during the long silence. Without looking at them directly she could sense them waiting, a blank wall of anticipation. But the receptionist outside was a magnet, drawing in Strand's unspoken thoughts and feelings. Strand remained equally open, almost providing a mirror.

"Well now, we mustn't keep you from your work."

"I really appreciate this chance to meet you," McKinnon said. "Broadcast is so interesting. You've done some fine work. Didn't you do that potato chip one?"

"No. But thank you, professor."

"Thank you for being so candid, Ms. Burroughs." Skinner smiled thinly.

Strand was soon back outside on the sidewalk. She didn't recall the descent in the elevator but she remembered saying good-bye to each of them, including Cynthia, the receptionist, whose name had slipped into her mind as she was listening. She remained in as open a state as she could all the way back to her office. Once there, she rested her head on her desk. Cynthia was wearing a wig, she thought, as she fell asleep for the better part of an hour.

SESSION #96

Nelson walked around the small living room listening to Strand. He picked up a miniature of the recently demolished Arc de Triomphe, and let his fingers run tenderly along its lines, regretting he'd never seen the real thing.

"You need to know they're suspicious."

"The Joneses are always suspicious."

"Nelson, don't. This could be your career."

"I get it, Strand."

"I don't want this to work for us and you end up with nothing."

"You know about my name, right?"

"It was your mother's last name?"

"No. It was my mother's first name. And her mother's before that. Over a hundred years. For this political leader who got put in jail in what used to be South Africa." *Mandela —"queering Africa"*

"I know."

"Just about everybody gave up hope he'd ever get out. Except a few who kept on petitioning and kept the fight going. When he did get out, the children he left behind, the partisans who were working for his freedom, they were all grown up. But they were still his children. They were different people but they were, somewhere inside, still the same. That's what I think will happen when we're done."

Nelson sat the small sculpture down carefully on a shelf alongside a tiny wood carving of an Ashanti stool.

"I want that moment when we look at each other and know, whatever the cost, we did something incredible, that nothing will ever be the same again. What is it you want from this, Strand?"

In the intensity of his voice Strand sensed Nelson weighing her. She chose her words carefully.

"I want to touch people," she said haltingly. "Not just seduce them into buying things, or be gawked at when we go to premieres."

She took a breath to begin again. "I never allowed anyone in when I was a kid. Too risky, you know. My mother was there one day and gone the next. I remembered her, did I ever tell you that? Not much: her smell, the way her shadow fell over me when I was in bed. Then she evaporated. Once dumped, twice shy. Then I met you and Lynx. Before that everyone was outside that glass."

"There are easier ways to break down barriers."

"But with this it's not just me. We can keep Lynx out of a hospital. Her work can go on, maybe even better than before."

Nelson could see Strand's thoughts taking shape as she was speaking. She was clarifying motives for herself as well as for him.

"This is not like Faust, or some shit like that, Nelson."

"I love it when you do the classics," he laughed.

"I feel like I'm sweeping up broken glass." Urgency rang in her voice. "I've got to do it, I don't know what to do once it's up off the floor, but we've got to do it."

Nelson said nothing. Strand remembered her visit to the DSS.

"You know Dr. Skinner thought we should be posting bans."

Laughter exploded from Nelson, the steeply angled light bouncing off the pristine shine of his head.

"I love your body, but I'm not that type of guy," he said through rippling giggles.

"Maybe we can use it to throw them off."

"All right, assume the position. You can think on it while I work."

He handed her the glass of tranq.

"Please just be careful, pay attention."

"Please just lay down, girlfriend. I'm doing color on front. Tell me about the trip to see the mother."

Strand recognized the worn contours of the table against her back. She stared at the ceiling, which was covered with a pale wash of colors, overlapping and delicately blended.

"Mae looks a lot like Lynx. Different hair, of course. But her body, her eyes especially. It made me wonder if she might be an empath too. Repressed empaths are pretty common, Lynx says."

She could tell from the hum of his machine that Nelson was too deep into the work to respond. Then her eyes closed. She thought not of the visit to Lynx's mother but of the first time she'd visited Lynx in a hospital facility where she worked.

It had seemed like fun when they'd first decided to do it, but once inside the lobby Strand only felt awkward and anxious. After growing up in an institution, she avoided them no matter what their purpose. She knew why as she waited for the elevator. There was a smell that marked institutions as alien, inhospitable to human life: the scent of decay, layered over with disinfectant and waste. The enforced crispness made all that was hidden more threatening. On the children's floor the atmosphere was only a bit more inviting than in the lobby. Strand had come because she could never picture what Lynx did and because Lynx had wanted her to.

"We can sit together on my break in about half an hour. Do you want to watch me?"

Strand nodded her head, curious about what she'd be watching, still unnerved.

"You sit in here. The mirrored wall lets you see. Just sit still, no swinging your legs or getting up and down. Alright?"

"Why do you work with the patients so late at night?"

"I think I'm strongest then. And they're freer, the air is quieter around us. It just works better."

Strand sat in an office chair in the small, darkened room and watched Lynx, wearing the yellow jacket with the bright red E Corps insignia, enter the room. She was followed by a nurse who wheeled a chair transporting a young Asian boy. About fifteen, he talked nonstop, angry words escaping him in spurts, aimed not at the nurse or Lynx, it seemed, but at someone not there. His swearing and temper didn't appear to perturb Lynx at all. Once helped onto the table by the nurse, he lay still almost immediately. The nurse, a tall, husky, middle-aged man, moved away, closer to the door.

"Alfred, you know why we're here, don't you?"

"Yeah."

"You know I want to help you."

"Yeah."

"I would never hurt you."

"Yeah."

"Do you want to be able to talk to the people you see around you?"

The young man was silent. His narrow frame twitched as if he were on a drug.

"Do you want to be able to talk to the people around you, like me and the nurse?"

"Yeah."

"Will you let me touch you?"

"Yeah."

"Will you let me touch the others you talk to?"

Again he was silent. Then, "Yeah."

Strand strained forward in her chair and watched Lynx lean into the boy, moving her hands slowly in the air across his body.

"You're really healthy, Alfred. Strong and smart."

Alfred was quiet as Lynx poised her hands in the air—one over his chest, the other near his head. She closed her eyes and slid into a slow, arrhythmic rocking. She bent in as if pulled toward him, held there and then eased away. The air around them shimmered, and out of the corner of her eye Strand saw the nurse gripping the door-knob behind him.

A spectrum of colors hovered and drifted as if carried on a breeze. They intensified as Lynx spoke.

"You keep yourself safe by talking to them, don't you?" Although her voice sounded relaxed, Lynx's body was rigid.

"Yes."

The pale shades deepened, becoming solid in the air, vibrating feverishly. Strand's eyes widened in disbelief.

"Good. Next time I'll talk to them. Okay?"

"Yes."

"Good." Lynx took a deep breath and Strand could see she was unsteady. The light receded, the colors evaporated. Lynx shook her hands out at her sides and touched the boy lightly on his forehead with a quick sweeping motion, as if she could rid him of his afflic-tion with a flick of the wrist. The boy watched Lynx closely while the nurse took his pulse and blood pressure. He made notes, then helped Alfred back into the chair.

"Thanks, Kevin." Lynx drew herself up straighter as Kevin started to wheel Alfred out of the room. "I'll walk back with you."

They disappeared from Strand's view, and it was another five minutes before Lynx returned.

"I never saw anything like that in my life," Strand said, trying to make sense of it.

"Children's Hospital is the easy shift." Lynx shivered as if she were chilled before continuing. "Alfred and I've been working for six months. This was a real breakthrough."

"He didn't talk much, but those colors—"

"He never talks to me!" Lynx interrupted, her excitement rippling through her exhaustion. "For months he'll talk a blue streak to those people in his head. And all I ever get is *yeah*. But tonight he said *yes*. I could feel it coming like a giant wave. He made a decision to say yes!

As she spoke, tears welled up in Lynx's eyes. Watching her, Strand understood what her work could do for the patients and for Lynx.

"I've got juice and snacks in my little room here. I need to lie down for a bit, do you mind? I wasn't prepared for this."

Strand didn't respond, but she knew she wasn't prepared either. She followed Lynx to a small room which held a single bed, refrigerator, lamp, and desk. Built into the wall was a monitor of some sort. When Lynx saw her notice it she said, "I can plug in there if I feel overwhelmed. Stereo!" She swept the headsets from the pillow, hung her jacket on the chair, and lay down.

Strand watched her breathing slow, noticing the soft curve of her breasts under the pale green sweater she wore. In ten minutes Lynx opened her eyes. Her color was back. She smiled as if she'd had all the rest she'd ever need.

"I can't believe it! Alfred said yes. You heard him!"

"He did."

"I can't wait to show the tape to the staff. I think Kevin, he's the nurse, has been doing what I asked. Keeping up conversation with Alfred even when he doesn't answer. Kevin was about ready to cry."

"The nurse seemed scared to me."

"I think everybody is a little scared of E Corps. We work together as a team—E Corps and a med staff member. Kevin's kind of new, but he's alright. He's really wanted to be able to help Alfred."

"Even I could tell something big was happening. Just the *yes*, I mean."

"Nelson won't believe it when I tell him."

"Nelson?"

"He came here. To see me work once."

"Really? He never mentioned it."

"Just one day after class, I think. He was curious. I happened to be working with Alfred."

Strand felt a twinge of jealousy—for Lynx and for Nelson. She couldn't unscramble the unfamiliar feelings.

"What happens now?"

"Kevin and I meet with the medical team tomorrow and present our report. If things go well, we get to work with Alfred more frequently. And we can start work on two other patients with the same presentation. There's a little girl, ten, I think, who talks nonstop; she has to be sedated to sleep. But she hasn't said a word directly to anyone around her since she was two. We want to begin touching her as soon as possible."

The assurance Lynx felt in her own world filled Strand with both desire and a sense of dread. Something in her life was changing, and she could not control it.

"I can't tell you how much I admire what you're doing." Even as she spoke the words Strand laughed at their formality. Lynx reached out for her hand.

"I want that from you. And more." Lynx's hand burned in Strand's. The connection was like a tunnel opening between them. Strand no longer thought of pulling away.

"Got to get back." Lynx met Strand's gaze.

"Yeah—I mean..."

They both laughed, then Lynx ended Strand's discomfort by brushing her lips softly across her cheek, then her mouth. "Much more," Lynx repeated in Strand's ear before she stepped back and grabbed her jacket.

Strand's eyes popped open and she was again looking at the soft colors of Nelson's ceiling.

"She's an amazing woman, Nelson."

"You betcha."

"I keep thinking there should be some other way to make her stronger, safer."

"I know the equation doesn't work out right. But look at her like the Joneses do: she's a commodity. Top shelf, but still a product that makes things run well. What do you think the Joneses would do to keep her in their store?"

Strand knew. She worked with people who sold products all day. The whole Society was one grand merchandising scheme. Society City and every town east of St. Louis was little more than a shopping mall. The health care Lynx gave was the property of the Society. If she could make a better profit for Society in some other city, some other country, or lying in a hospital bed, she'd be sent there to do her duty.

Strand left Nelson's, eager to curl up in her own room to get away from these thoughts.

SESSION #112

The evening was cool as Lynx and Strand walked toward Nelson's flat holding hands, something they rarely did in public. A small bronze figure sat in the shrubbery just before his building.

"And who's this supposed to be?" Lynx asked, aware of the gaps in her education.

"Rodin. I hate Rodin in miniature," Strand answered. "Claudel's better anyway." They both laughed. They didn't ring the bell but stood together looking around them at the lawn and the pieces of sculpture. Lynx held on more tightly to Strand.

"Are you alright?" Strand asked.

"I am. It's just every day I go to the Correctional Hospital and I don't know what to expect. I'll be happy when we...when I don't have to go to any of these places. Broadcast, the hospitals."

"Soon. Try to hang on."

"I know. Maybe it'll be a relief to do the work somewhere else, without them holding my leash."

"We'll do it together."

They laughed again and rang the bell.

Upstairs, Nelson had chilled a bottle of champagne and opened his door with an exuberance matching theirs. A jazzy harmonica played an old pop tune through the stereo speakers as Nelson settled Lynx and Strand in chairs with glasses. He sank down into a large pillow on the floor. They looked at each other silently for a moment.

"I'll stick to water," Nelson said. "Don't want to make any railroad tracks."

"Only a little for me. I'm going to the hospital from here."

"Looks like you're carrying the weight, Lynx."

The silence returned. In the time Strand and Lynx had known each other, spending hours in Nelson's flat or at Ruby's, words had never been this difficult for them.

"I got the present you two brought back, but Strand never told me how it went with your mother," Nelson said. The tiny replica of an old-fashioned tractor sat on the bookcase, the deep grooves of its oversized wheels next to the delicate whitewalls of a bright yellow antique car model.

"It was good, I think. Mae was relieved to see me, and she loved Strand."

"You're kidding?"

"Hey, I thought you were my friend."

"Strand, honey, you know I love you but I don't think you ever called yourself a mother's delight."

"She was crazy about Strand," Lynx protested. "If Mae could find a man like Strand she'd be remarried in a minute."

"You go a long way between singles bars out there." Strand sipped from her glass.

"There's a lot of Partisan activity in that region these days, working roads, like that," Nelson noted.

"Partisans?" Strand asked.

"Some of them rebuilt a fence for Mae once and did some other stuff. Four women traveling together, kind of working their way around the countryside, doing chores for women who needed it, bartering for food."

"Partisans?" Strand repeated, unable to decipher the meaning of the waver in Lynx's voice and hating that she felt so much like Society wanted her to feel.

"Don't believe everything the Joneses tell you, Strand. I keep reminding you of that."

Strand didn't respond. She rarely accepted Society's word on anything. She saw for herself, too closely, how it was constructed, deconstructed, and embellished. She was frequently one of those polishing up the words, making them go down more smoothly with citizens. But if she totally rejected Society, what did she believe in instead? That was where she always stopped when she thought about it. Having Nelson in her life had given her the promise of something else, something hovering nearby. Learning how to care with Lynx had drawn it in even closer.

"Partisans are all different kinds of people, Strand. Women who want to live away from men, men committed to end militarism, greeners. They do their own work, their own way. Sometimes missions overlap," Nelson continued.

"If we go west, we'll be seeing Partisans, Strand," Lynx added cautiously.

"You'll be needing Partisans."

"Time for the fun part," Lynx said before Strand could respond. They all clinked their glasses together. Then, as Nelson reached up from the floor, they put down the champagne and held hands.

"Hey, this is a grand adventure, remember?" Strand said.

"It's working, isn't it?" There was no question in Lynx's voice.

"Yep. I can feel the differences."

"Let's make a toast then." Lynx raised her glass again.

"To?"

"Art and magic?" Strand said.

"Art is magic." said Nelson.

"Art is magic." They touched the rims of their glasses together a second time and sipped quietly until Lynx rose to leave. Strand felt a rush of affection and of fear as Nelson embraced Lynx at the door. When this was done she'd never see them together again. Was escaping the Society really a possibility? Was it worth losing this camaraderie?

After Lynx left, Strand and Nelson settled easily into their task.

"Did you ever notice that you rub your head just before you start working? Every time."

"Um-hum." Nelson nodded.

"Up or down."

"Down, I'm going right to the collar and cuff edges.

"I signed out on sick leave this week."

"It's time. Tranq?"

"Just a little." She sipped from the glass Nelson pulled from his refrigerator.

"Good to go?"

"Good to go."

He clicked on the machine, not expecting much conversation tonight. Strand stared at the wall nearest Nelson's kitchen, which was broken by a wide pass-through and a counter with stools. Above the opening, tacked to the walls, was a series of drawings—she and Lynx alternating, each subtly different from the one before it. She closed her eyes, no longer needing to see the images; she remembered what Lynx had looked like when they'd first met and now she knew almost every line of her body.

Standing in the field which was part of her mother's small farm, Lynx spread her arms, mimicking the tree behind her. Strand watched, fascinated by the difference being on the farm had made. Even on the drive west, before they'd been outside Society City for an hour, Lynx had started to appear less burdened. Here in the field Lynx's skin was luminous, the furrow of anxiety had disappeared from her forehead, and her laughter no longer had an edge of hysteria. Even Strand herself felt different. She was kindly toward the livestock, the grass, even toward the neighbors who occasionally lurked at the end of the long road leading up to the house, hoping for a glimpse of their own local E Corps oddity.

In the quiet of the field, her arms raised to the sky, Lynx looked to Strand much as she had in the childhood pictures Mae had shown her over dinner.

"Do it," Lynx said.

Strand mirrored Lynx, raising her arms to the sky, closing her eyes.

"Keep listening. Everything you could ever want is right here, all around us."

Strand took the air deeply into her lungs. Her body wavered slightly, then she felt the caress and support of the light breeze. The leaves sounded like a river moving overhead. Insects swooped and darted. A pungent farm smell hung in the air, as did the soft sound of cows nearby. Lynx and Strand did not touch but stood adjacent, synchronous and harmonious, their bodies like similiar outfits on hangers in a department store.

Energy tingled through the air around them. Rather than straining, Strand relaxed into the sensations. Then the memory flooded her: Mae brushing her hair. For almost an hour as Mae hummed, then talked about her own mother. The feel of Mae's hands on her neck and head was comforting. The soft bristles of the brush sweeping across her scalp, pulling through long red curls, was firm and reassuring. Further back in the memory Strand sensed not only Mae's enjoyment but her fear. Just as Lynx had described it.

Strand dropped her arms and opened her eyes. She thought she'd cry but no tears came. Lynx put her arms around her and spoke softly in her ear, "You can feel my past now, can't you. Like I feel yours."

Strand had no need to answer.

"Mae fought her fear, that's the courageous thing," Lynx said.

"They were all afraid. Society's still afraid."

"That's why they're so dangerous." Lynx's voice had the authority Strand had heard in the hospital, and an edge of determination. Here among the trees Lynx was solid. She was an extraordinary but natural force in the world, not a commodity.

"There are other things I hope you never have to feel. But I don't know that I can stop it."

Strand watched sadness fill Lynx's eyes.

"At the Prison Hospital. They deem some prisoners incorrigible."

"Who deems?"

"Some committee or other—the Joneses. They keep reporting the crime rate is down. Everybody's happy. Nobody wants to know."

"Know what?"

"We...the E Corps...we touch them. If we go deep enough inside and pull back we can take back their feelings."

Strand was silent, trying to understand.

"We take back all their feelings. They can't hurt anyone, ever. They can't do anything. Soon, without the feelings, they seem to die on their own." Shame flooded Lynx's voice. "Each time it feels like it's killing me, too."

Strand pulled Lynx to her. The breeze turned chilly with the set of the sun; they trembled in each other's arms.

"You cold, girl? You got goosebumps." Nelson drew Strand back to the present.

"I am a little."

"I'll jack up the heat." He turned the control on the floorboard heater. "I'm about done for the day."

"Really?"

"You've been laying out here more than two hours!"

"I can't tell anything for sure anymore. Disoriented is beginning to be my middle name."

"Look good on a marquee."

"The other day, before I filed the papers for my sick leave, I sat in on a department meeting. Everybody was throwing out ideas for a new campaign, some music group the Society's pushing—kind of English, kind of rock, a little social conscience thrown in. They're doing an international release. So I suggested we use an underlay of John Lennon footage. The room went silent, like I'd just spit on the table."

Nelson kept his eyes on the work, but he could tell the usually hard lines of her voice were soft. Her mouth quivered slightly as she told the story.

"The exec says, 'The guy's been dead over a hundred years, Strand. Who's gonna relate to that?' That wasn't really what topped me off. It was the damned producer. Twenty-five years old. He's heard five rock'n'roll sides in his entire life. He says, 'Forget Lennon. Wasn't there something about him and God?' Can you believe that?"

"Cogs in a wheel have fuzzy memories."

"But can you believe it! He knows as much about images as a turnip. I didn't know what to do. I wanted to slap him on his head. I leaned over, looked him in the eye, and said, "God who?" and walked out. I've never done that before. The Broadcast producer almost had a coronary behind me."

"Nothing's the same anymore, honey."

"Then, when I got to my desk...I cried!"

"Take it easy. Don't be trying to take on the whole world yet."

"Lynx keeps saying the same thing."

"Are you going there tonight?"

"Lynx says we're having a romantic dinner. Do you think that means vegetarian?"

"Nope, chocolate."

"Are we on for tomorrow?"

"Let's hold up for a day, okay? I want you to get some rest."

Nelson sprayed the newly worked-on sections and watched Strand tentatively put on her clothes, as if all of her energy had been drained away by remembering Broadcast One.

"I'm gonna walk you over."

"You don't have—"

"Nix. Let's go." Nelson opened the door and grabbed one of his several voluminous garments from a hook by the door. They walked side by side to the corner in the cool evening air. When a jitney arrived they got in and rode silently across town.

Nelson stood on the sidewalk waiting for Strand to enter and go up in the oversized industrial elevator. He glanced up at the window when he heard the final clang. As he turned away he saw, out of the corner of his eye, an old pair of running shoes suspended by their knotted strings from the street lamp. He smiled, pulled his large cape around him, and walked toward Ruby's.

Once upstairs, Strand let herself into Lynx's flat and laughed with joy at Lynx's preparations. Champagne glasses gleamed on a low coffee table alongside colorful paper napkins and plates. In the refrigerator were several small dishes with pickles, paté, cheese, and a couple of things Strand couldn't identify.

The dog, Sliver, followed her around hoping for a treat, while Dot watched from her perch on the top of the stove. Strand, suddenly exhausted, lay across Lynx's bed. Her mind whirled with pictures she couldn't shut out: co-workers she'd said good-bye to casually as she went on leave; Lynx's mother, Mae; the road west they'd driven to get to the farm. Her head started to feel achy. She considered taking a pill until she noticed that Sliver and Dot were stretched out around her. She closed her eyes and sank back into the comforter. Sliver and Dot nuzzled against her, one on either side, and Strand's thoughts slid away into a pool and swirled around each other until they'd drifted into the distance.

Strand opened her eyes an hour later to see Lynx standing at the foot of the bed, watching her. Sliver and Dot sat up, waiting for her attention.

"Are you hungry?" Lynx asked. "These animals sure are."

"I'm sorry. I should have fed them when I came in. I was just so wiped out I had to lie down."

"How are you feeling now?"

"Like I'm getting over a migraine."

"You keep still. I'll feed them and come back and join you."

Strand lay back on the pillows, enjoying the sounds of domesticity from the other room. She listened to Lynx turn on the shower, then opened her eyes again to see her standing nude in the doorway, her damp hair wrapped tightly in a knot at the top of her head. The rounded angles of her hips and arms seemed a little firmer. Her normally tanned and freckled skin was pink from the heat of the shower.

"I feel better now." Strand's voice was both langorous and eager.

Lynx helped her out of her clothes and knelt above her on the bed, aware of the tenderness of Strand's skin.

"Not as good as we're going to feel," Lynx said before their lips met. Straddling Strand's body, Lynx grew more excited. Their mouths pressed together, Lynx touched one of Strand's breasts. Lynx moved down the bed and licked at the lines and colors on Strand's belly, hip bones, thighs, knees. She nipped at the hairs that protected Strand's mound and then pushed her tongue inside. The taste was almost salty. Musk filled Lynx's head as the sound of Strand's joy filled the room. They both understood this might be their final time. *how sad & awful*

They slept lightly and awakened in the predawn hours, finding each other's bodies again before sinking deeply into sleep.

The next afternoon, Strand called into her office to be certain no final details had been left undone. She already felt as if she'd been away for months instead of days. Her only regret was not saying a real good-bye to Freda. When Lynx went to the hospital in the evening, Strand sat looking out the window of the flat onto the street of warehouses.

Strand found it odd that Freda should come to mind so vividly now. Memories of tasks they'd done together filled most of Strand's evening as she sat quietly with the cat and dog, wondering why it was her secretary and not her job she missed. She stretched out on the couch and closed her eyes. When she started to drift off, she felt another presence. Strand lay still, listening, and realized she was sensing Lynx, just as Lynx was listening to her.

Strand's breathing slowed, and she sank into a state between sleeping and waking. She perceived Lynx's thoughts and activities at the hospital as if she were by her side. When Lynx went in with a patient, Strand could feel the lights in her head rather than see them as she did when, through the mirror, she'd watched Lynx work. Her body felt hot but not uncomfortable. When Lynx pulled back from touching the patient, Strand felt the release and was tired as Lynx rested before treating someone else.

When Lynx got home she found Strand lying on the couch as she'd been all evening. Lynx fed Dot and Sliver, then sat in the kitchen listening as they ate. The one other living space in the building was empty; a warm quiet lay upon the building. When the animals finished they followed Lynx into the living room. She led Strand to the bedroom and helped her undress. Dot and Sliver waited at the foot of the bed until the two women climbed under the comforter. They lay in each other's arms with the cat and dog inched into the spaces around. They all slept dreaming each other's dreams.

SESSION #124

The sun seemed unable to pull itself from behind the clouds. The air in Lynx's rooms was mired in dampness, but no rain fell. Strand paced the flat, confined and irritable. Lynx prepared for her final days at the hospital. She noted Strand's dour mood but didn't question it. She asked Strand to make tea for them. Sitting at the small kitchen table, they held onto their cups as if they were life rafts.

"Did you say why you'll be out?"

"No." Lynx shook her head. "I alerted Kevin so he could make alternative treatment schedules. I didn't say anything, just smiled conspiratorially. I think he thinks I'm doing something juicily il-

loaded w/ issues : capitalism ← Corp.Am.
                                            Healthcare
race
sexuality/orientation
segregation
"Big Brother"   130 ◆ DON'T EXPLAIN

licit." Lynx smiled at the thought and went through the list of all she'd accomplished.

"I've brought my notes on patients up to date. I managed to get a consult with someone in E Corps for each of my patients so no one will be left without a professional who has an interest in their case. I haven't done deep work in a while so no patient has to be really disrupted by a new link. Kevin's good, Strand. He'll make sure treatment is followed through."

"My work was so easy to leave. No consequences, no meaning, really." Strand's voice was deflated by exhaustion.

"It had meaning to you. The visuals, creating images."

"We'll see what that means in the long run. It seems petty compared to healing."

"Art is magic. All art," Lynx said. "If we lose that, we're back where we started—carving out replicas. We're both working for a government that's a corporation. Crime, health, advertising. It's all the same." The edge in her voice was new, raw.

"Have I got a Partisan on my hands now?"

Lynx smiled as she stood to go to the hospital.

"What time is Nelson coming over?"

"Not 'til seven."

"Get some rest."

"I think I will."

"I hear Mount St. Helens is quite lovely." Lynx tried to cheer Strand.

"Then perhaps we better see her."

Strand paced the flat after Lynx left, feeling restless and tired but unable to lie down. She decided to go out for a walk and found herself, unexpectedly, on the street of her own flat.

She went in and looked around as if they were the rooms of a stranger. The walls were covered with framed images. Glossy magazines sat in stacks around the couch and on the dining table. The bookcase held a few more magazines and awards she'd won for advertising jobs. There were three heavy lucite discs sitting in bronze bases. Small plaques celebrated past campaigns she'd developed. Strand packed them in pages crumpled from magazines and nestled each carefully in a shoebox. She wrapped the boxes in plain paper from one of her pads of sketch paper and addressed each in elaborate script: for Freda; for Truong, the elderly messenger; and for Buster, who'd been her driver whenever they went on location. She wrote *thanks* and drew ornate borders around their names, grabbed her two favorite ink pens from a drawer, and shut the door behind her. She took a jitney to Broadcast One as she had for the past eight years. She left the packages with the night guard and boarded another jitney to Ruby's. As she neared the brightly lit window, Strand felt a rush of warmth at its familiarity.

Once inside, Strand wasn't sure it had been a good idea. The cafe was bursting with people. Dishes, glasses, and voices clattered in her head. Ruby waved her over.

"Sit at the bar with me," she said, recognizing Strand's distress. She poured a glass of wine and watched as Strand took a sip.

"You don't look like you should be wandering around alone, my friend."

"I guess not. I'm not feeling so well."

"Danny," Ruby called behind her. A muscular, dark-skinned man with mixed gray hair appeared in the swinging doors. "Will you give Nelson's friend a lift?"

"Sure. Be right back."

He disappeared back into the kitchen.

"I can get a jitney, Ruby."

"No, girl, you look too out of it. You don't want to see Nelson angry with you or me."

Danny reappeared five minutes later wearing a cap and sweater. He took Strand's arm as if he'd done it countless times before.

"Okay, little lady, we'll have you comfortable in no time."

His voice was soothing; its low pitch and even tone easily lulled Strand. She remembered little of the ride back to Lynx's flat. She didn't even remember telling Danny where to take her. He parked and walked her to the door.

"Tell Nelson I said hey," Danny called over his shoulder as he turned back to his car.

Strand lay down on the bed, Sliver and Dot at her sides, until she heard Nelson ringing the doorbell. He lugged his massage table inside and set a large bag on the floor.

"You look like you haven't slept since I was here last!"

"I think that's about all I've been doing." Strand hated the whine creeping into her voice.

"Well, girlfriend, this is gonna be it."

"You think?"

"It better be. DSS was at my house yesterday." He tried to sound casual but Strand heard the anger; she was surprised she heard no fear. A knot formed in her stomach.

"Don't worry, I've been keeping the machines in another spot ever since they called you in."

"If they confiscated your wonderful old machines, the Rogers, the Cindy Ray...."

"It's okay, they're safe." Nelson set the table up in the middle of the living room. "I've been prepared for this."

"What'll happen when we're gone?"

"Make the stereotypes work, honey. I'll be a public nuisance, grief and abandonment dressed in feathers and red, the hysterical victim of a calculating advertising bitch. Then drop into the background. Everybody will be so happy that the big, black queen shut up, things should quiet down."

Anxiety kept Strand silent.

"I'm not leaving town. That would put DSS on me like a tracking bug." Dot rubbed against Nelson's leg and then against the table's.

"Find a seat, puss," Nelson said firmly as he pulled a premixed bottle of tranquilizer from his bag. Dot crossed the room and sat on the back of the couch.

"You've got the touch," Strand said, "with the cat, I mean."

Nelson beckoned her to the table.

"This is going to be in your face." Nelson laughed. "It's mostly shading, no fine lines. But you need to concentrate. And relax at the same time. I really mean relax. I've got options if something happens here. And you'll see me on your doorstep, if they have such things in the wild, before you can say silk and satin."

"Should we...I wondered...what..." Strand wasn't certain what question to ask.

"We'll just proceed like we always do. I'll work on your face and neck for a couple of hours, if you can. Then come back later and do your hands."

"I thought we were going to do it all at once."

"We'll see. The face work is more shadowing than anything else, but that's delicate. The hands are detail. We'll see."

"Can—" Strand started.

"Quaff!" Nelson handed Strand the bottle.

Strand took a sip and grimaced. "What is this—a double dose?!"

Nelson didn't answer as he set out colors. Strand put her clothes across the arm of the sofa and lay on the table.

"Up, I assume."

"Yep," Nelson said and clicked on the machine, enjoying the delicately balanced weight in his hand.

"It's going to be fine, Strand. Just open up, let things in."

"Look who you're talking to."

"I am looking." With his other hand he brushed the softness of Strand's face. Her lips curved in a smile under his hand. Through the tips of his fingers he felt her surrendering to the tranq.

"It's odd working here. Everything is right and wrong at the same time."

"Shhh."

Strand's body softened against the table, the hypnotic buzz of the machine filling her head as Nelson leaned toward her face. The vibrating of the needle was a large and frightening sound for a moment, then Strand was in darkness and the sound was her only reference point. She clung to it briefly, letting it go to make room for memory.

She waited outside the hospital for an hour before going in to see what was taking Lynx so long. Remembering the way from her visit several weeks earlier, she went up to the children's floor. She couldn't figure out what to say, what approach to take, so decided to do what she always did: act like she knew. It would conceal her fear that something had happened to Lynx.

Emerging from the elevator, she found her way back to Lynx's resting room and opened the door quietly. The room was empty. She walked in and unlatched the refrigerator. Bottles of water stood neatly alongside an unopened packet of cheese. Strand stepped back into the hall and closed the door.

She looked around, trying to blank out her uneasiness at being in the hospital, at not finding Lynx. She'd decided to talk to the floor nurse back near the elevator when she saw Kevin coming toward her and was relieved she remembered his name.

"Hello, Kevin, my name is Strand. I don't know if..."

"Oh, sure..." The smile of recognition faded, and the angle of his body and his silence told Strand something was wrong.

"I'm looking for Lynx. She was due to get off over an hour ago."

"She had to leave." Kevin looked as uncomfortable as he had the night Strand had watched him through the mirror while Lynx worked on the young patient.

"What does that mean, Kevin?"

"They...I mean she was ill. We were working with one of the children. And she slipped."

"She fell?" Strand felt overwhelmed by information she couldn't decipher. The place, his words, all seemed a jumble.

"No. Come inside, that'd be better." She and Kevin stepped back into Lynx's resting room. Kevin and Strand were the same height, but his bulk made the room and Strand feel small. He leaned back against the door in the same way he had when she'd first seen him: holding onto the doorknob behind his back.

"She slipped...off center...I guess is the best way to explain it. I don't know how much you know—"

"Just tell me what happened, I'll figure it out."

"She slipped off center. Her touch was not simply reaching inside the patient—she was losing herself. She insisted on finishing with this one patient. She's been working a lot. Too much, I think, in the last couple of months. She just wanted to finish up so the kid could go on to the next phase of treatment."

"But what happened, exactly?"

"I took the girl back to her room. When I didn't see Lynx, I came back to the treatment room and there she was, standing, but completely unfocused. Like she was unconscious, but standing." Kevin's voice shook with emotion. Strand could see why Lynx had such faith in him.

"I know the procedure: I just eased her onto a gurney, strapped her down, and covered her with a blanket."

"Strapped her down!" Strand couldn't keep outrage out of her voice.

"So she wouldn't fall out. That's the procedure." Kevin's tone asked Strand to understand. "Then I called the E Corps officer. We're not supposed to touch any member of the E Corps. I took her pulse, though. I had to...to see what I could. It was very slow, slower than anything I'd ever felt. But she was in there, I could tell. Then they came."

"Where'd they take her?"

"I don't know. This has only happened twice the whole time I've been here. Both times they brought them back to their resting rooms, but they bundled Lynx into a van. They wouldn't even talk to me. Just made me tell them everything that had happened in the session with the kid. And afterward. I'd already started writing my chart notes. They took them away! Can you believe that shit? I've got to write them out all over again for the kid's file."

"They took your notes?"

"They flew out of here like they were going to a fire. But I tell you she's going to be fine. I'm sure of it. She was pulling it back together, she just needed time. I don't know why they—"

Strand turned abruptly toward the elevator, then turned back quickly. "Thanks, Kevin. I'm sure you're right. I'll just go by her flat. Thanks."

Strand rushed back to Lynx's, not expecting to find her there but disappointed that she didn't. She sat heavily on the sofa, about to call Nelson, when she realized the cat and dog were watching her. She almost rose to feed them, then stopped. They were staring at her intently. This was different from their customary longing-filled gaze. They sat side by side across the room, their pupils slightly dilated.

She decided to do what Lynx was always suggesting—she listened. She opened up her awareness and heard the room, the space around her. She gazed at Sliver and Dot, who were sitting more still than she'd ever seen them. Noise from the street did not disturb their attention. Then she heard Lynx, a slow surfacing of thoughts inside Strand's head, as if they were her own.

I'll be fine. There's only one way. Steady. Close down. Shut out all.

Drugs run their course. Close down. I'll be fine.

Strand sat on the couch as if paralyzed. The thoughts were coming to her from Lynx, she was certain. She didn't know what to do. Tears started to roll down her cheeks and she touched them, puzzled.

She woke in the middle of the night, her head resting on the back of the couch and a dull headache clouding her memory. Sliver and Dot were still sitting side by side, but facing the door. A few moments later it opened and Lynx came in. She seemed so deflated that Strand almost didn't recognize her in the dark.

"What does it mean?" she asked Lynx.

"I had a hard time holding on to my focus. The closer we become, the more difficult it is for me."

"Why?"

"I can't explain it. Think about yourself, Strand." Lynx's voice was weak, with an undercurrent of urgency. "You keep yourself under tight control most of the time. You haven't given a thought to anything but work, the machinations of Broadcast One, for almost ten years. No real life, or friends, except Nelson. And he takes you exactly as you are, without making demands. You don't do any charity work, don't go through drama with friends, don't sympathize with anything."

Strand's head was pounding, but she could hear that Lynx's words were said in sadness, not anger.

"Sit, let me," Lynx said, and waited for Strand to sit back on the couch.

"You're a wonderful woman, Strand." Lynx held her hands close to Strand's forehead. "But it's buried very deep inside. You've got armor on your armor. That's why it scared you to know how much I cared for you. Then you had to open up to me. And once you *really* do, all kinds of things can happen. And that scares you. If you're not the Strand you used to be, who are you?"

"Things are better."

"No, I'm losing strength, Strand. Every night at the hospital I'm less focused. And they notice."

Strand was chilled to the core. She grabbed Lynx's hand which almost glowed with heat. "I won't let them take you away!"

The next evening Lynx did not work and they arranged to meet

Nelson for dinner at Ruby's. The answer came to them there as they listened to him talking about a tattoo he'd done ten years before: the heart of a lion on the breast of a young woman.

"I logged onto a med library. Finding full-color zoological pictures of internal organs is no easy slide, let me tell you." Enthusiasm was fresh in Nelson's voice. "It was perfect—aorta, ventricles, veins—full color. And she needed it, you know. She was just at a place where she could leave some garbage behind; this was the push she needed. A couple months later, when she came by my place to say thanks, I could see the difference even before she said a word. She was filling out her...her self, like she wasn't even there before. I been tattooing ever since."

Strand and Lynx glowed with a frisson of understanding. The tattoo was more than the symbol: it was the essence. In their mutual weaknesses they could complete each other.

"Strand. Strand?" Nelson's voice was distant and slow as if he were talking through mud. When she opened her eyes the light's glare forced her to close them again quickly.

"Sorry." Nelson moved forward to block the light. "You were a little too still for my tastes, girlfriend."

"I was remembering that night at Ruby's when you told us about the lion heart tattoo." She squinted to see the outline of Nelson's shining head.

"You two got the heart." He clicked off the light. "Okay. You're really doing great. I'm gonna hold up here for now. I'm not spraying your face. You ain't going nowhere, are you?" He laughed as he said it.

After helping Strand up he folded his table and put it in the corner, cleaned his instruments, wrapped them in cloth, and slid them into the deep pockets of his long coat.

"What time will Lynx be home?"

Strand looked at her watch. "Not 'til much later, she's going on break about now."

"Don't touch anything. Let Lynx work on you when she gets in. Just a little. Not too much."

"Yes, sir."

"Wish I could have that answer on tape. Tomorrow, the hands,

7:00 P.M."

Strand lay on the bed, the animals next to her. She didn't fall asleep until just before Lynx came in, moving quietly through the rooms, feeding the animals, taking a shower, before approaching the bedside. Holding her hands over Strand's face, Lynx worked slowly, first letting the heat build, then releasing the energy. Strand lay still without speaking.

"I can almost see it," Lynx said, "but don't look until later."

"I don't need to look. I can feel it, inside. He finishes tomorrow he thinks. The hands."

"I know." Lynx took Strand's hands in hers and kissed each finger. She rolled her tongue around them, sucking, tasting, enjoying the way they pressed against the inside of her mouth. The evening in Ruby's seemed very long ago to both of them.

Lynx pressed Strand's hands to her breast, waiting for their heartbeats to return to normal. Then they lay side by side until the next afternoon.

SESSION #146

Nelson set up the table and puttered around the room, unsure how he wanted to proceed, uncertain in a place not his own. He glanced at the drawings of Lynx and Strand pinned to the wall and smiled. He liked his work.

"I'm not worried," Strand said. "Not anymore."

"I didn't think so. Maybe I am. You'll be on the move. I'll have to come out to the boondocks to visit. Ugh!" He shivered in exaggerated distaste.

"Perhaps you know some Partisans you'll be wanting to visit."

"Mebbe, as my great-grandfather used to say."

They both looked around the room, knowing it would be the last time they saw it in quite this way.

"I'm going to have you lie down as usual, since that's how we're used to working. But I'm going to rest your arm on the dining table, okay?" He spread towels on the table as he spoke. Strand sipped at the bottle of tranq, then climbed on to the table with a familiarity she was sure she'd miss.

"Nelson."

He looked up from the colors he was mixing.

"I don't know what to say, I guess."

He strapped the needle machine to his hand. "You'll get a package in a couple of days, with information you'll need once you're out of the City. Lynx's mother's farm will be the contact point if you have any problems. But then you'll just keep going west 'til you decide to settle down. Partisans will help."

"Sounds so simple."

"It is and it isn't. And I'll want a postcard."

"I know, I know. It's not just the lack of people on those landscapes, is it? It's the possibilities. Open space, not corrupted, no one trying to sell you something.

"Sounds good to me."

"Then you better come out west."

"And who'll help out the folks back here?"

Strand relaxed, feeling the animals watching from the other side of the room. The machine clicked on.

"You know I've only been mad at you once, all the time we've been friends?"

"Um-hum. No talking now though." Nelson leaned forward and the glare of his light washed over her arm. Strand closed her eyes, remembering the last time Lynx had been hospitalized.

She waited at home for several hours, expecting Lynx to call. She tried the hospital, then Lynx's home. Then she decided to sit and listen as she'd done before, but nothing came through. Since they'd been working on the tattoo they were entwined, inseparable, even when they were on opposite ends of town. Each had become a soft hum in the other's mind, a slight vibration under each other's skin.

Strand didn't understand what was happening. She leapt up from the couch and slammed out of her flat, running toward Nelson's. When she rang the bell she realized it was late, but he buzzed her in without asking who it was.

As she walked in, before she could speak he said, "I know. She'll be alright."

Something in his voice stopped Strand.

"How can you know that?"

"She should have stopped working earlier. Things are too fragile right now."

"How can you know any of this?"

"Sit down. I'm sorry we didn't talk about this possibility. She just had an episode."

"She slipped." Strand did not sit down.

"Yes, she slipped. Not good, but not totally uncommon. She should not have been doing such deep work while all this is going on."

Strand's eyes narrowed as she looked at her friend. She was increasingly uneasy and not sure why his words weren't comforting. She repeated her question.

"You know, don't you. Just like Sliver and Dot know."

Strand stalked across the room. It looked odd without the massage table at its heart. She turned at the kitchen and stared again at Nelson.

"You're one too!"

His eyes and hands were unnaturally still, Strand noticed.

"You're an empath too!" Strand almost screamed. "Why were you hiding it—from me?" She twisted around as if looking for something to break, then collapsed against a stool at the counter.

"I've hidden it all my life, Strand. I never wanted to be forced to fight the Society to have a life. Whatever healing I do I do on my own."

"You've been my friend for how long?" Strand moved in closer.

"We've been working on this project for over a year. You couldn't tell me?"

"You won't know what it's like to be owned by the State until we're finished with this project. Even then it'll be a memory, not the life you live every day. Lynx knows. And I saw it happen to my best friend when I was fourteen." Nelson pulled his caftan around him protectively and glanced at his shelves filled with its tiny toys. "We planned to visit all those places that don't exist anymore. Old tourist spots. We figured the vibes would be wondrous. We were inseparable. Finished each other's sentences. Wore each other's clothes.

Knew how to comfort each other. I loved him.

"Then E Corps took him away. After that he made one visit back to see his parents—he hardly spoke to them. Or to me, when I showed up. I could feel him struggling to make sense of us, so many other voices and lives were inside him. It was like we were all ghosts in some former life he'd had. Then he split for good.

"It wasn't until he was gone for almost a year that I figured it out. It wasn't just him. It was me, too. Without me, he almost couldn't handle it. I shaved my head so no one would know—and I stay repressed so other empaths can't find me."

"Why couldn't you tell me, once we started working?" Strand could feel the tears of betrayal welling up inside her.

"To explain in words isn't that easy, Strand. I know that's part of what we're supposed to do, that's why they gave us the education, the training. But sometimes words just don't explain anything."

"Does Lynx...of course she knows. Doesn't she?"

"When she walked into the class it was like I was knocked off my feet by a gale-force wind. I'd kept everything clamped down, except when I did tattooing. Then I tried to help people, kind of like Lynx does at the hospital. But by the second session she was speaking to me in my head. We both knew we were going to do something wonderful. We weren't sure what, but then you kept asking about her. And she wanted to meet you."

"You two planned this!"

"No. We never planned anything. We felt our way to it. Untangled the mass of confusion and connections, and here we are."

Anger nudged against Strand until she kicked it away. They hadn't tricked her; everything there was to know they'd revealed.

When you're not blocking us out you hear.

Strand heard Nelson's voice in her head. The round tones she'd listened to for hours calmed her now.

"It's really going to work, isn't it?"

"It is working. You made the choice, Strand. A good choice for both of you."

"It's like you're someone else I don't know."

"No, it's just that now you know me better. As my great-grandfather used to say, 'What real queen shows all his cards at once?'"

Queers more open?

"Your great-grandfather knew more than any great-grandfather I ever heard of."

"He was queer too! Didn't I ever tell you that story?"

Strand opened her eyes as Nelson sprayed fixative on her hands. The lines of shading on her forearms and the backs of her hands were subtle, even before healing. Nelson watched her face. Her approval pleased him.

"I don't know how much better it could be. I feel like I'm always telling you to relax. But a major ingredient in healing is rest."

"Nelson...I love you."

"I knew you could do it. Now let me have one final look."

Strand stepped out of her tunic and pants as Nelson turned the light onto her full body. She stood as still as Lynx had done in their class when Nelson circled her, looking at the lines he'd drawn, the coloring he'd added.

Each joint, fold, wrinkle delicately matched. Lines and perspectives balanced. Colors blended. Strand stood as if she were a grand Maori woman warrior, the worlds inside of her mirrored by the fleshly lines. Nelson had never done such an extensive tattoo and was amazed himself by the impact. As he watched, the lines seemed to shift and flow with a life separate from Strand.

"What about the wheels?" Strand said, alarmed as she remembered the bicycle tattoo on her calf.

"Not to worry. We've got it covered."

Strand decided she was done asking questions. Nelson walked around her one last time then said, "See you on the trail, sister."

"Not before we leave?"

"No. Always." He pulled the table out into the hall, then kissed her forehead.

"I feel like we should say something more."

"We're not saying good-bye."

"In the orphanage, all those people I grew up with—the kids, the counselors—they came and went like lights blinking on and off. They're a blur to me. Even the people I worked with every day at Broadcast, I could barely remember them or their lives when I wasn't in the office. That won't be true with you, Nelson."

"We do get to pick our families, Strand. And we picked. We picked good." He reached out and held his hand in front of her face, almost caressing her cheek. Heat flowed between her healing skin and his palm. He closed his hand and a cool breeze drifted in as he picked up his bag.

Strand listened to the elevator descending, clanging and squealing as usual. But nothing felt usual. Once Nelson was gone, Strand was listless. She'd always been proud that she was going into middle age in good condition. But the past few months had worn her down in ways she couldn't account for. She was determined not to be in bed when Lynx came home this last time. She sat at the dining table and read a book, turning the pages gingerly.

Lynx came in earlier than on previous nights and found Strand asleep with her head down on the table, the book her pillow.

After taking her shower she stood over Strand, admiring the work Nelson had done on her hands. She held her own hands out beside them, and her breath caught. She woke Strand gently.

"I have to show you something."

"Ooh. I'm sorry I fell asleep."

"It's late, of course you're asleep. We'll both be soon. But look." Lynx pivoted on her foot to display her calf. On it was a fresh tattoo—a pennyfarthing which matched Strand's. The large, spoked wheel, delicately connected to the smaller wheel behind, curved with the muscles in her leg.

"When'd he do that?" Strand said, excited. "How'd he do that?"

"Tonight. It was alright! I was fine the whole time!"

Strand was amazed that Lynx could bear the needles long enough for a tattoo even this simple.

"Let's go to bed." Lynx nudged Strand from behind. Her long hair, still wet from the shower, left a string of droplets across the floor, which Dot pounced on.

They lay in bed in silence until Dot and Sliver jumped up on either side of them. They all dropped off to sleep. Strand woke for a moment just before dawn, but Lynx was not in the bed. She tried to hear her in the other rooms. It was silent though, and before Strand could call out, she was asleep again. They both slept through the next day. In the late afternoon Strand got up to close the curtains against the sunlight.

"Are you hungry?" she asked Lynx, who watched her from the bed.

"No. I..."

"I'll feed Dot and Sliver." Strand started to leave, then sensed something. "What is it?" Strand couldn't conceal the alarm in her voice.

"I can't move...I don't think."

In one leap Strand was kneeling beside the bed. "What—?" Her voice was strangled with fear. Lynx lay on her back, arms limp by her sides.

"It'll be okay, I think." Lynx's breathing was shallow. "I just... remember those old television shows we saw once? They used to take people's molecules apart to transport them somewhere, then put them back together? Remember how we laughed?"

Strand only nodded.

"My skin is prickly, like needles all over. It feels like my molecules are moving. Away from each other."

Strand sucked in her breath, trying to decide what to do.

"Nothing. Let me lie still and see what happens. Go do the food."

Strand reluctantly went out to the kitchen to feed the animals. By the time she returned, Lynx's entropy was dispelled. She'd curled into a ball and was sleeping. Strand crawled in, spooned around her, and the two women slept again into the night. Dot and Sliver didn't join them.

Lynx awoke sometime after midnight, relieved to feel her limbs returned to normal. She got up to look out the window. She pulled the curtains back and let the streetlight shine in, smiling at the pair of shoes hanging from it. Nelson had told her to look for that sign wherever they went.

Lynx turned back to the bed, where a shaft of light from the window spilled over Strand. The new lines on Strand's face were already healed. It was amazing yet natural to Lynx. Strand shifted under the sheet, restless but deeply asleep. As she did, Lynx started in shock. Strand's arm, which lay on top of the sheet, was almost transparent. The wrinkle of the bedding underneath was outlined almost perfectly—through Strand's arm.

Lynx snapped the curtain shut, terrified. She continued to watch

Strand, now barely visible in the dark, and took long, slow breaths until her pulse returned to normal. After a few minutes she realized she was too sleepy to stand any longer. Lynx returned to bed, slipped gingerly under the sheet, and was asleep before she could reach out to touch Strand. As she fell more deeply into sleep their dreams overlapped.

Light lifted from their bodies and swirled around as if on a giant disc. Their light, all the shades of it, spiraled until it blurred. Lynx turned and rustled in the sheets. Strand lay still, her body sapped of strength. Through the night the spiraling and spinning swelled in their dream until it was a sound filling their heads. The whirring grew, engulfing the room. The light that rose from their bodies formed an arc above them which, in turn, was drawn into the spinning colors. Lynx turned onto her back, Strand onto her stomach, then back again. And they dreamed the turning until just before dawn.

They lay facing each other. Lynx opened her eyes first, then Strand. Lynx stretched and rolled onto her back, extending her arms; Strand slipped into her embrace. They explored each other with their eyes closed—hands, mouth, skin—each savoring the feeling of flesh on flesh until they could feel it no longer. The sensations of two became one.

When the sun was full in the sky, beating hard on the closed curtains, Dot and Sliver jumped onto the bed and settled themselves around the sleeping woman.

The doorbell rang at noon. Its insistence was as startling as the sunlight pouring through the bedroom window. Dot and Sliver danced around each other, hungry as usual, and excited to have company. Sliver even gave a small, rare bark.

"Be right there." She struggled into the tunic laying across the chair, grabbed the knit cap from the dresser, and pulled it on.

"Package for Tryna Nelson West," the voice of a messenger called through the door.

"That'll be me," she said as she swung the door open, pulling her clothes down behind her. The messenger, a young woman with bright, eager eyes, grinned as she held out the gaily wrapped package.

"Happy Birthday!" she added.

The woman looked puzzled for a moment until she saw the wrapping. Her hazel eyes widened. "Wait, please." She turned back to the living room and rummaged for a tip.

The messenger watched the woman, whose golden skin seemed to glow. The coloring was puzzling to her—the woman's features seemed African but her skin was tawny and freckled, almost Irish. Her green knit cap was bursting with hair.

"Here we go. I'm sorry to keep you waiting."

"That's okay. Can you sign here?"

"Of course." Tryna Nelson West wrote smoothly, with little flourish, as if she'd been signing her name for years.

"Thank you." Tryna reached out to shake the messenger's hand. The girl responded automatically and was startled by Tryna's electric touch.

"Thanks." Tryna's voice was deep with laughter sparkling behind it. The messenger pulled herself back from the hypnotic smile and said thank you as she took the tip Tryna offered. She glanced back over her shoulder as she waited for the elevator, to get one last look at the woman who seemed to be so many things at once.

Tryna closed the door and stretched, trying to recognize her body. It was both familiar and alien, forty and at the same time young. Her squared fingers seemed the most recognizable. She went into the bathroom and gazed in the mirror where she saw colors and characters not blended but annealed. The tattoo lines were gone and each of the women existed whole, inside and beside the other, in one body. Tryna turned and saw on her left calf the freshly drawn pennyfarthing, the only part of the tattoo still healing. Anywhere you want to go.

Turning back to the mirror, she pulled the hat from her head with some anxiety. As she dropped it to the floor a flood of pure white dreadlocks fell around her face onto her shoulders. The bathroom light bounced off her shining hair as if in protest of its incandescence.

Tryna smiled into the mirror as she recognized herself. Both parts were there.

"We better get ourselves packed," she said to Dot and Sliver who circled behind her. She walked around the living room, wondering what she'd want to take. She opened Nelson's package, examined the train ticket, map, and new birth certificate. His face looked back at her from a self-portrait done in pencil. It was protected in a plastic sleeve with a handwritten letter she decided to save until she was on the road. She took down a picture of Mae, the drawings of Lynx and Strand, and put them all together in the envelope. She packed it, along with some tunics and caps, into a duffel bag she found in the closet.

Sliver ran around the bag and Dot tried to crawl inside.

"I'm not going to forget you guys, don't worry. See?" Tryna pulled their two soft carriers from a hook in the closet. The animals leapt and whirled in excitement.

"But first let's eat. I'm starving."

They ran eagerly before Tryna to the kitchen, then sat by their bowls to wait.

Tryna turned off the light in the bathroom; she didn't need to look anymore. *Anywhere you want to go.* She listened to the day around her.

✦

HOUSTON

*W*ind—soft, cool, and sweet—was perceptible only to Gilda as it flowed through the shadowed grotto. She closed her eyes and sniffed the air, listening. In front of her, leading back to the surface, was an empty corridor of stone, damp with the silence of underground. Behind the wind she heard the stealthy steps she'd noted earlier. The sound advanced purposefully toward her— it was not a random spelunker, but a hunter. She stepped quickly into the bend, behind a shelf of rock. She was tired of being hunted and sought only to leave the cave, to go into what was left of the city for her share of the blood. She was even more eager to find a safe place to unroll her pallet and rest before dawn.

The cautious tread brought the hunter closer as Gilda scanned the blackness, calculating how to move past him and out into the night. It was a ridiculous strategy, but tried and true: she crouched down, and as the hunter stepped around the bend she stuck out her foot. He fell, splashing into a fetid pool of water. Gilda reached down to render him unconscious, almost smiling at the comic picture of her potential kidnapper sprawled on the ground. She de-

what she wishes to do to critics

cided to take her share of the blood from him and, in exchange, leave him with the thought of pursuing another profession.

But he shot her. It was as if he'd been expecting the fall. Without turning over he simply twisted his wrist and fired wildly. His narco-dart grazed her shoulder; numbness immediately settled on her skin. Within a second her shoulder joint had turned to stone. Her fingers still worked, but she couldn't raise her right arm at all.

The hunter leapt up, astonished that he'd actually wounded her, but his eyes filled with fear as he saw that she did not collapse as he expected. Gilda struck out with her left hand; it was equal in strength and speed to her right. She sent the hunter—a square, ruddy man—flying across the cave into the jagged wall. Even in the dark she could see the sheen of biphetamine in his eyes. The drug made him quick and merciless, eager to make his capture and take his pay for her life.

Gilda heard the hunter's breathing and pulse rates quicken in both anticipation and terror. Her own slowed to a steady pace as she poised to turn. Although the numbing stopped at her elbow, she was not certain if the narcotic effect of the dart would allow her to move quickly enough to become invisible to the eye. The narrow passage of the cave was a trap, but it was her only recourse.

At the same moment she decided to risk flight toward the dark-ness she saw the dart gun move into position. This time he had her, she thought. Then a hard breeze and a mild whistling sound rippled through the cave. The hunter crumpled into a heap, the kind that can only mean death is present. Her eyes flooded by shock, Gilda turned toward the breeze and saw a man in the shadows.

"He was going to kill you," the man said simply, as if he could hear her mind protesting death. He stepped forward. His thick, curly hair, tied back in a ponytail, revealed a broad face with sharp fea-tures and dark eyes.

"No, he would have only incapacitated me, then sold me."

"That's about the same as killing, I think," the man said, moving to the dead hunter.

"It is sometimes worse," Gilda said, thinking of the haunted look she'd seen cross her mother's face so many years ago, and in the eyes of many other slaves on the Mississippi plantation. It was a look

being like a slave

she'd been afraid she'd see in the mirror one day. But she'd escaped. That was two centuries in the past, yet the fear of being hunted still coursed through her veins, embedded in the life-giving blood that kept her young. She watched the man bend over the body, turn it, and from the wound pull a short sword—the wind Gilda had felt whistling past her. The sword's delicate silver handle gleamed even in the darkness of the cave.

"I don't like to leave him here," he said. "Sometimes children come out to explore, or—"

"Yes, let's bury him properly," Gilda said. Anger tinged the edge of her words, an anger she experienced when anyone, even a hunter, invited death foolishly. She moved to the man's side as he wiped the bloody blade on the dead man's pants leg.

"There's a clay deposit just further in. We could dig a little, or maybe use rocks."

"Fine."

Gilda helped him hoist the body, using her good hand. They walked almost a kilometer into the cave and found another alcove. There was a small depression, and the man's body fit easily as they each labored in silence, piling rocks onto it. Gilda was relieved to see that the man did not rifle through the dead one's pockets; he worked solemnly as if this were a personal duty. She tried not to listen to his thoughts—they seemed too private right now—but she wondered what he did with the killing. Did he keep the man's face inside himself as she'd been taught to do? She knew few mortals who took such care any longer.

The silence echoed with their work. Rock and dirt fell with a dullness that sounded secret and ominous. Gilda sensed the man's eagerness to speak as well as his hesitation. She thought only of finishing the task and continuing on her way to find the blood she needed.

"My name's Houston," he said finally. "It's H-O-U-S-T-O-N, but like HOUSE. Houston."

He stuck out his right hand to shake, but Gilda's arm still hung leadenly, her right side pulled down by its weight. He switched smoothly to his other. When their hands clasped, Houston looked at Gilda fully for the first time. Her grip was granite hard but her

[handwritten margin note: why proper burial]

like empath

dark skin was soft. As he gazed at her it became clear why the hunter had been after her. The steely strength of her arm was contained but unmistakable. Her dark eyes swirled with a liquid orange glow.

Gilda felt his mind flood with confusion as he, through her hand, *mind read* felt her heart. It was calm, not malevolent or voracious. Nothing for him to fear. He was able to sense those things—just as all of those on his mother's side of the family could do. He knew he stood holding the hand of a vampyre.

"You've nothing to fear from me. I would not take your life even if you had not just saved mine."

"You read my thought?"

"I can, when necessary. Whenever I'm in a dark cave with a man I don't know, who carries a short sword, I try to read his thoughts."

They both laughed, Houston somewhat incredulously, but again like those of his mother's family. He enjoyed a good wit.

"I am Gilda. Why are you called Houston as in "house" and not Houston as in the old city?"

"It's after a street in the place that was New York. It used to be a major thoroughfare."

"I've heard of it," she said softly.

"When my mother's family escaped from Poland, they opened a little restaurant. A delicatessen?" He looked at Gilda, making sure she understood the old term.

"Yes, I remember New York City, and I remember delicatessens and *boulangeries* and *taquerias* and theatres and cafes, and all the things that had wondrous names before the government mandated only English words could be used in public spaces," she said impatiently.

"Well, her mother's mother, twice removed, opened a place on Houston Street and it was just called EATS. They served all the food her mother had taught her to cook, just like the old country. My mother used to hear the stories about it when she was young. There was this war, in Europe..." He trailed off and looked at Gilda as if she were from another planet, not familiar with the history. She nodded, remembering the war some had chosen to forget, or pretend never happened. She let him see the memories in her mind; the death and terror he'd only heard about were cold images deep inside

like terrorism

her. He stood paralyzed by the magnitude of the small flash of the past that swept through him. Then he was himself again, as Gilda loosened her influence over him.

"First it was mostly those from our country, Poland, then others. The restaurant never turned anyone away, whether they had money or not. Sometimes they'd eat a meal or sandwich and then wash dishes or hose down the sidewalk. Or they'd just eat if that was all they could do. My mother used to tell me the stories, and she'd have tears in her eyes as if she'd been there. Full of pride, you know. She used to say, 'Take just enough and give as much as you can.'"

Gilda listened to the rhythm of Houston's voice and heard others she'd known before—Sorel, Anthony, Bird. Voices of those she called family, the ones she was searching for now.

"I was her first. She named me Houston, so the story would stay alive, I guess."

Gilda looked at the man, hard and direct, as if she would pin him where he stood.

"Actually, it's David Houston Klepfisz." He answered her look of disbelief.

Gilda said nothing. Her mind was full of the pictures of New York as she'd last seen it, trying to imagine the teeming community of Polish immigrants, refugees from the horrors of war.

"I was lucky she didn't name me EATS, huh?"

Their laughter rang off the walls of the cave. Gilda was fascinated by the man's light-hearted nature. It had been so many years since she'd been with her family; his stories made her ache. She rubbed her shoulder, trying to hurry the feeling back into it.

"And your generous mother? Where is she now?"

"She died ten years ago. I suppose she was lucky, she lived to be forty."

Sadness crossed Houston's face. The world had turned into a burial ground for the mortals. He still had a healthy complexion, and she didn't hear any wheezing in his lungs. To Gilda, he looked to be about thirty. Chances were he'd be dead, like most mortals, by forty or fifty.

"I have to ask you an open question," he said.

"Yes?"

Holocaust
revenge

"You don't kill? You take blood, but you don't kill someone who's hunting you, to sell you?"

"Killing is not my way. Not the way of my mother's family. When I take my share of the blood, the sharer does not die. And I do not kill when any other option is available."

"Then come with me. I know someone who can help with your arm."

"My arm will heal itself in time."

"I hear the government's been experimenting with even more toxic weapons. You can't be sure what damage has been done. My friend lives in the Jemenez Mountains just to the north. She's a witch and knows herbs."

A surprised laugh escaped Gilda. "I don't think I'll be needing a witch."

"Ah, a disbeliever. How'd you feel if she said she didn't believe in vampyres?" Houston said with a smile. "You must've known people with powers, healing, things like that."

Gilda thought of Marie LeVeau, the vodun priestess who she'd only heard about as a young girl when she'd lived in Louisiana. And of those who'd given her life. Their lives were rich with powers, but she'd never call them witches.

"I know those who can speak without speaking," Gilda said cautiously.

"See. My friend, Archelina, can hear voices of people who aren't with us anymore. She was very famous among her people in Iowa. Too famous. So she moved into the mountains here."

Gilda's heart pounded. In the passing centuries there'd been so many losses; what voices might she hear through the witch? But the hunger was rising in her. Her time had come a while ago. She could no longer ponder the past; she needed to reach the city and find the one she would share with before the night became much shorter.

"I can't make that journey now. I...I must go to share the blood soon." She was surprised to hear herself speaking the words aloud. "It's not good to wait too long. The hunger becomes a deep pain."

Houston watched, fascinated by the orange light swirling in her eyes, and saw the way she strained to compensate for the dead limb at her side.

[handwritten margin notes: "Told society need Lesbians feed off each other — balance"]

"I can't meet your witch. I must go," Gilda said, sorry to leave Houston behind.

"What about me?" It was out of his mouth before he thought. He looked embarrassed as he sputtered, "I'm healthy and your handshake says you don't lie about killing."

"I will not give you my blood." Gilda was suddenly wary. Was this open-faced young man scheming for ways to prolong life in these unhealthy times, tricking her into the very trap he'd saved her from? She peered into his eyes and saw his thoughts: helping her. And something else: loneliness. He wanted company, someone to laugh with. Gilda had not thought of herself as a mirthful companion, but it was true that they'd made each other laugh.

Gilda pulled his consciousness into her mind, wound it slowly into a tiny ball, and put it to the side. She spread before him a green sea of grass so he felt comfortable as she lay him down on the rocky cave floor. As she leaned over him his eyes closed peacefully. She sliced through the skin on his neck just below the line where his beard would be growing back in. The flesh was soft, the pulse steady. The line of blood was deep red and familiar as it welled to the surface. She pressed her lips to the warm liquid before it could spill down to color Houston's gray shirt.

The ferrous scent, sweet like sea air, filled her nostrils. She took it in and let the blood satisfy her need. How odd, she thought, to take the blood from him—a stranger, yet not a stranger. His dreams were not anonymous. Their pulses merged as she drew the blood in; his breathing slowed to meet hers. Gilda listened inside him, sifting through to see what hope or dream she might fulfill in exchange as was her duty. She could feel he was a man of great principle and kindness, much like her friend Sorel. *Friend.* The word sprang from him into her mind. In saving her, his need for friendship was reawakened. But what could she do to give him a friend?

Gilda took no more blood. She rested Houston's head gently on the damp ground and stood, preparing to leave. He would wake, find her gone, and go on with his life, she mused. But what of her part of the exchange? She'd left nothing behind for him. Gilda listened to the distant sounds—slow drip of water, echoing wind— and thought of the dead hunter who'd tried to take her into captivity. He would have made a small fortune selling her to one of the rich ones seeking to escape the short life to which mortals had condemned themselves.

The limestone water in the puddles around her was now reflected in the tainted rivers and oceans around the world. Only in the caves was the air ever moist and cool. Since the turn of the century the millions of laborers, teachers, clerks, and others who lived from day to day had given up hope of health. That was reserved for the wealthy. The hunter would have retired on the money he'd received after selling her—to be kept barely alive and transfused repeatedly until the buyer felt certain he, too, was immortal. Then death for her. Cleaving her head from her body. Or burning, like they used to do to witches.

Houston started to revive. The power of his blood shone in her eyes as Gilda looked down at him. Beside him his short sword gleamed with the care he so obviously lavished on it, yet by his blood Gilda knew that violence did not lead his heart. *Friend* was the only word she heard echoing inside him. As the world had grown more desperate, the idea of friends had become more precious. Few had room for it in their hearts. Even those who'd suffered at the hands of the rich often sought only to become despots themselves.

"Come, my little delicatessen," Gilda said with a smile as she reached down with her good hand and helped him up. "Let's go visit your witch."

They traveled in Houston's hovercraft until the sun began to show itself. He then guided the craft into a ravine, covered it with brush, and set an alarm. They entered another cave, much like the one they'd left hours before.

"How's the arm?"

"Numb. I'll rest till afternoon. Then we travel again."

Houston was uncertain what to do but said, "I'll keep watch here at the opening."

"Good. Please don't come to look for me."

"Uh, no, I'll be right here." He set himself up, back against a wall, just inside the mouth where he was hidden from anyone approaching. Gilda passed into the recesses of the cave.

Just as the sun passed its highest point in the sky, Gilda emerged from the darkness and found Houston still sitting erect against the wall. He leapt to his feet, surprised at the light cloak she'd fastened over her head which kept her face in shadow. They wordlessly reboarded the craft and traveled for most of the day. Gilda thought and Houston talked.

The highway they skimmed was overgrown and cracked. Few people ventured this far outside the city, yet Gilda sensed life in the brush. There were some encampments, and occasionally she saw a lone figure walking or on a motorcycle. They encountered no others in hovercrafts. They arrived at the Jemenez just at sunset, and Houston took them on foot through arroyos and along brambled paths until they were within sight of the mouth of a cave above them.

Here they sat as Houston explained they must wait for Archelina to acknowledge their presence and invite them in.

Gilda stayed enraptured with thoughts of her past. And of the future. This world she'd seen for so many years had become a festering sore. In all of her almost two centuries of life she'd never held as much fear as now. Everywhere she turned there were fakers and charlatans cloaked in numerous guises, promising the dying population salvation. They saturated the broadcast channels and weighed down street corners. Some wore spiritual robes; others wore suits that signaled their sanctified prosperity; but no one asked the population to think about what was happening closest to them. In fact, their promise of salvation was making the poverty, illness, and pollution invisible—or at least someone else's problem. One that could be ignored as the populace reached for some higher state of grace and affluence.

Gilda had struggled for years against despair, a by-product of the perspective afforded by her long life. She remembered the cities Houston spoke of nostalgically, the laughter of people standing on the streets, the wonderful buildings all looking different from each other. And the beauty of the old people.

In late afternoon, before dusk frightened them inside, the elderly had often walked through streets arm in arm as if surveying their long lives. Gilda would look into their finely crafted faces, smiling at the ones with light still shining in their eyes, knowing she would never wear the crown of silver or feel the soft folds of fleshy age draped around her. It had been many years since Gilda had seen anyone over fifty.

Gilda didn't know what she expected to happen when she met Archelina, and was uncertain why she sat among the sparse grass and cactus waiting for a light to appear in the mouth of a cave several hundred yards above them. She felt pulled by more than just Houston's enthusiasm and sense of humor but had no desire to wrestle with some revivalist selling false ghosts.

Gilda stopped questioning herself and pushed her attentions outward in a circle that widened back down the mountainside. She scanned the surrounding area methodically to see what other life was near, determined not to be surprised by another hunter. She was interrupted by Houston's shout.

"There she is!" Houston jumped to his feet eagerly.

"Yes, I see." Gilda peered through the darkness. The woman standing above them was broad, filling the space illuminated by the oil lantern she held aloft. Her skin was the brown of clay and her hair stark white. It was in two long braids which ended near her knees in bright red. At first it appeared to be fabric wrapped around their ends, but on closer inspection, Gilda saw that the lower half of the braids themselves had been dipped into a henna. And her eyes were milky white, unseeing.

Houston had already started up the rocky path. Gilda followed, quickly overtaking him.

"It's been a long time since I've been here. But she always remembers. Even before I open my mouth."

In his excitement Gilda heard the child he'd once been and an enthusiasm that had been lost to this world. She patiently kept the pace Houston set—hurried for him, snail-like for her. She settled inside the rhythm of the fifteen-minute climb, listening to the air around her as they ascended and the light from the cave grew larger.

When they finally arrived they took the lantern Archelina had hung at the entrance and walked deep inside, uphill toward a chamber that lay higher. They entered a large space draped with cloth and animal pelts. Thick cushions were set on ledges and the floor of the cave. At the center was a huge wood-burning stove whose chimney seemed to feed directly, incongruously, into the stone above. Archelina stood in its glow holding a loaf of bread and a knife. The fierceness of her face suggested, on first glance, that either might be a weapon. But then she smiled. "Houston. I wondered if you'd ever return."

"I told you, I'll come here to die. Nowhere else."

"The way you wield that short sword, you may have little choice about where you die."

"Are you saying I have no skill?" Houston's retort rode on laughter as he lay his gleaming weapon on a shelf of rock by the entrance.

"I'm saying you live too much with those who find your skill a challenge and don't treasure life as you do." She turned her head as if she were peering at Gilda, but the blindness was complete.

"Gilda," she said, "good to finally get to meet you."

Shock coursed through Gilda. "You know of me?"

"Yes, and some of the others."

"They've been here?" Gilda said, barely containing the excitment in her voice. This witch might be able to confirm she was following the right path, reuniting her with her family and securing their escape from this dying world.

Archelina walked to the round wooden table that sat to one side of the room, touching its edge gently, and started to slice the bread.

"No. They passed on the other side of the mountains."

"May I ask how you know?"

"I listen."

Archelina looked as if she were anywhere from sixty to one hundred years old. The skin of her face was full and healthy even where it was wrinkled. Her hands were large and strong as she sliced rapidly through a loaf of wheat-and-corn bread. Her broad frame was unbent, although Gilda could sense the delicacy of the bones. For the first time in her life, Gilda stood before a mortal with natural powers perhaps equal to her own. It made Gilda feel both comforted and anxious. And something else Gilda was unable to grasp: she could not read much from Archelina's thoughts. It was as if they formed only at the moment they left her mouth and entered the air.

"Whenever I find myself in a cave with a man with a short sword and a vampyre, I always shield my thoughts," Archelina said aloud.

Houston and Gilda both looked startled. Then the three of them laughed, letting the ringing sound bounce off the walls for much longer than the slight joke warranted. It was a laughter of recognition and of bonding.

"Gilda took one of those narco-darts. Just a graze, but will you examine it?"

"You don't really need my help," Archelina said as she held her hands in front of her, stretched out, taking in the aura surrounding Gilda. "Not with your arm. That has already started to heal itself. Remarkable."

Heat suffused Gilda's face. She wasn't certain if it were a response to Archelina's uplifted hands or just to Archelina.

"Will you let me touch the place to feel the healing?"

Gilda walked closer and turned so that her numb shoulder was beneath Archelina's hands. They rested in the air just above Gilda.

"Oh my, yes, how remarkable. That's how it's done, is it?"

"I don't really know how it's done. Our bodies heal themselves, we don't grow old."

"The legend is true then. I thought it might be, but the wealthy create so many fantasies."

"You know there's a religion based on it now," Houston said. He sat back on one of the cushions as if he'd reclined there often. "Everlasting Life, Inc., or something like that," he went on. "People pay a lot of money and some guy in red robes claims to be over a hundred years old and tells them about miracles he's done, always in some other part of the country."

"Not anymore," Gilda said.

"What do you mean?" asked Houston.

"I...communicated with him recently. He now feels the need to work only at the bedsides of those with little time left."

"You took blood from him?" Houston's voice was full of impatience.

"And helped him remember his original impulse."

"You could change the world, you know that?" Houston said angrily, as if Gilda were trivializing her powers.

"Only in small ways. Not everyone is as easily persuaded to return to their original path."

"She's already changed the world," Archelina said. "These small ways are what often make the difference."

Gilda again felt a spread of warmth, although Archelina had returned to sit at the table. She was wearing loose-fitting cotton pants wrapped tightly at the calf and ankle. Gilda watched as Archelina crossed her leg and noticed her feet were quite small. They, unlike anything else about her, made her appear vulnerable. Archelina leaned forward and turned toward Houston. "It's not like you to reach for quick fixes."

"There's nothing quick in this!"

Gilda saw the fierceness that lay inside Houston for the first time. Much of the laughter that flowed from him sprang from a well of hurt and anger.

"There's been no immune booster medicine for generations. People gave up on fresh water before the turn of the century."

"And it will take generations to undo any part of it," Gilda said in a soft voice.

"And while you talk of generations, people we love die around us."

"The change must come from within, Houston. No one can impose the idea of justice. Before science can cure, people must want it, must demand it."

Archelina held her hands clasped in her lap. She spoke tenderly. "We know these things. Houston sometimes forgets in his enthusiasm."

Gilda watched the exchange, fascinated by the interplay of emotions—the love between them, Houston's anger and fear, Archelina's concern both for him and for her own mortality. As they sat, Gilda felt her own body come alive with a desire she found startling. It rose from deep inside her and pressed against her center. She wanted to lay with this woman, feel her body close to her, smell her sleeping. She missed that simple pleasure more than she realized. Archelina raised her head as if she'd just caught Gilda's thought.

"I must go out," Gilda said.

"Why? Are you afraid?" Archelina asked.

Houston looked from one to the other, sensing the tension between them and understanding it immediately. Instead of uttering his usual joke, he rose and started to spread jam on the slices Archelina had cut. He filled his mouth with bread.

"I don't know what you want from me," Gilda said to the old woman.

"To help, in a small way."

"What help do I need?"

"Do you truly wish to know that?"

It had been decades since she'd felt the need for anyone's help in any profound way. But now, what were the questions swirling inside her? More than simply what road to take. Where to find her family and make a new life would be revealed when the time was right, when everyone was in their appropriate place. What could she really need from this woman who stood before her like both a comforting grandmother and an irresistible siren? What was in those hands that drew her?

"To visit the past," Archelina said, with a hint of surprise in her voice.

"No!" Gilda almost shouted. "I don't need to revisit the horrors of enslavement. The dead remain so!"

Gilda's uncertainty about her surroundings, and who might have followed her and Houston, fueled her words. It wasn't safe to disappear into some kind of spirit trance, searching the past with so much unknown right outside.

"Your vehemence implies a questioning. We can't wait for a safe time to ask questions." Archelina turned to Houston as if she could see his form. "You are her friend now. What shall we do?"

"I'll clear the table," Houston answered. He stood to remove the bread, jam, and knife. Gilda watched as he and Archelina prepared for a ritual that they had clearly performed more than once. Houston used a clean cloth to scrub the table, then went into a smaller chamber which lay behind the main room. He emerged with four large branches. Gilda recognized scrub pine but did not know the names of the others. They looked to be from local trees. He laid the tree limbs upon each other in the center of the table. The three of them stood at the table silently for a moment.

"Tell what you remember," Archelina said to Houston, as if intoning a prayer.

"I remember when water and the eyes of the people were almost clear. I remember soil full of life and the energy that healed from inside. I remember the idea of justice. I remember many mothers and fathers who remembered many mothers and fathers. My mother's touch and the words she sent to me after she died. And I remember when we gave each other shelter. Tell what you remember."

When Houston finished his recitation, he and Archelina drew closer and extended their hands to Gilda. She reached out, turning her palms upward as they stood around the thick brown circle of wood. They held hands, completing a circle.

Archelina spoke: "I remember when the sky, water, and eyes of the people were mostly clear. I remember fields reclaimed, and harvests. I remember the old and the young."

A frisson coursed through Gilda's body as if it were dividing it in planes. Some parts were present; others were floating alongside, feeling the experience, not seeing it; and others rose above her and watched. She lifted her head and looked up to the ceiling of the cave as if expecting to see herself there. Instead she saw the constellations painted in a soft white. Where the fire threw light she recognized the stars of the fall sky. Small dots and fragments of cloud were painted in perspective off into the darkness. She looked back at Archelina and wondered how she accomplished such artistry, or if it were Houston's handiwork.

"And," Archelina continued, "I remember to provide shelter." As she spoke, her already erect body stretched and turned in the light flickering in the open grate of the stove. The room filled with shadows that seemed made of light itself. Houston's face glowed with joy as if he were seeing or hearing something that was just for him. Archelina's brow furrowed in concentration. She rocked her head back and forth forcefully, her long braids falling first in front, then behind her. With each swing toward the table her breath was expelled in a whisper. A knot of anxiety pulled across Gilda's chest. Archelina looked as if she were going to fall across the table. Then she stopped the distressing movement and turned toward Gilda.

"I don't remember any words." The voice from Archelina croaked with effort. "It's much too far in the past for that. I remember deep love. Sorrow. Profound exhaustion. Indignation. Anger at injuries. Love is still here. Tell what you remember."

Gilda picked up the memories which were, in fact, her own. "I remember muscled arms, first in rough cotton, then others in fine velvet dresses. Rouged cheeks and sad eyes. I remember how it felt to be lifted to safety by her." Gilda's voice cracked as she squeezed her eyes shut. Dry sobs broke through each memory.

"I remember how she drew the despised to her, no one cast out... how she loved us. Her blood flows through me...she's gone...I remember. I remember to offer shelter." The last words were pulled from Gilda's trembling lips like an unexpected covenant. As she said them she knew her path had turned.

"I remember," said Houston.

"I remember," Archelina said, drawing her hands into her lap and holding onto her braids.

"I remember," Gilda echoed. A burst of cool air filled the room as if working its way from the past into the present. Gilda stood immobile, her head thrown back, her eyes finally open but her gaze sweeping the ceiling of the cave sightlessly. Tremors rippled down from her head to her shoulders, arms, and hands. Archelina and Houston, with Gilda in tow, swung their clasped hands into the air. At the height of the arc their hands separated and a swirl of air and light flew above their heads and disappeared into the painted sky. Gilda finally looked around her but nothing seemed changed, except the fire in the stove had burned down quite low.

"Now we eat."

Houston brought the bread back to the table along with some cheese and a plastic container of wine. Gilda and Archelina sat quietly while Houston went back into the chamber and returned with glasses glistening with colors.

"It's in his blood, you see. To serve food. He's inherited that from his mother's people as well," Archelina said.

They sat around the table. Gilda sipped at the heavy red wine, watching the others eat hungrily, as if the experience had sapped their strength.

"I love seeing my mother's face. She didn't speak this time," Houston said.

"Soon she'll be completely diffused, absorbed by other energy."

"I know," he said smiling.

"And what of you?" Archelina asked.

The remembering was individual, private. Each of them had their own visitation which Archelina facilitated but did not recall.

"The one who made me has been gone for so many years, only the feelings were left to remember."

"That may be the most important part."

"They were fervid. Her convictions all-encompassing. She cared so much for others, for me. In the end the caring wore her down," Gilda said softly. Then she added with some surprise, "I could see that I'm not near that end at all."

"Everyone has their allotted time. Years or centuries."

"That's a relief in so many ways."

"Why's that?" Houston asked, leaning forward across the table.

"A sense of time can make things more precious, more—"

Gilda broke off and Archelina held her hand up abruptly at the same moment.

"Someone's below."

Houston leapt to his feet and started toward his sword. Archelina stopped him with a slight movement of her hand. "No killing!"

"It's probably a hunter," he said to Gilda, "tracking us from the southern cave. Maybe they're working in pairs."

Gilda listened more deeply, then turned back toward the opening. "I'll see to it." Before he could protest she added, "Stay here with Archelina."

"Your shoulder?" he asked, but Gilda had already disappeared through the opening into the darkness.

She moved quickly down the corridor of stone, listening as she went. This one used more caution than the other. His movements were not steady but erratic, hard to track. He stalked her as if he had all the time in the world.

Gilda steadied her attention on his silence. Sound echoed around him, bouncing off and concealing, rather than exposing, his movements. Gilda listened to the waves. When she focused around him— the dripping water, the wind, the rustle of animals—she could pinpoint him.

She took a position in the center of a corridor and probed his thoughts: calculation, sport, only the prey on his mind. She sensed the presence of some type of stimdrug, but not a biphetamine. This hunter counted on his prowess rather than narcotics. Gilda fell back into the shadow and began to rattle things in his mind. She moved rocks and shuffled in his imagination so he followed a path almost directly to her. She pulled back even deeper until she felt the cool limestone through her tunic. As she did she realized Archelina was by her side. Gilda almost gasped in shock but could not; her throat was locked in silence.

Archelina leaned close to Gilda's ear. Her breath was warm, sweet with corn as she said, "I'll speak with him. No killing." Archelina loosed her hold and Gilda was able to respond. But she was unsure what to say. There was no room for contradiction.

The footsteps of the hunter advanced as they stood motionless. Gilda saw Archelina raise her hands slowly and felt a warmth surround her. The hunter stepped around the corner still in shadow, cautiously scanning his surroundings, attack-ready. He made his way directly toward them. Gilda wanted to raise her hand and signal that they back away, but it wouldn't move. Archelina turned her head to signal no, and Gilda stood almost paralyzed as the hunter advanced. Then she heard Archelina's thoughts: He can't see us, we're cloaked. Wait until he is just here. Then you may touch him as Houston has told me you do.

The hunter now stood less then two yards from them. He turned and should have been able to see them both, but his eyes brushed past as he continued down the path. Just as he was within arm's reach Archelina dropped the cloaking that masked their presence. The hunter realized something was amiss and Gilda kicked the narcogun from his hand. Archelina rendered him unconscious by simply raising her hand higher. Gilda stepped forward and caught him as he fell, laid him on the rock, and quickly removed his other weapons, throwing them into the enveloping darkness. Archelina stood beside them, unseeing yet knowing, her arms still outstretched. She'd turned her palms downward, her fingers spread almost as if she were playing the piano.

Gilda knelt above the hunter, uncertain—she'd never taken blood with someone nearby, so cognizant. She could find no reason not to, so leaned in and sliced the flesh at the hunter's neck. Archelina's sharp intake of breath reverberated in the darkness as the blood seeped out. Gilda drew the warm red into her, relieved this hunter would not die. She touched his mind, his heart, seeking what it was that he desired beyond profit. Survival seemed to crowd everything else out of his mind. There were few aspirations for him beyond making the capture, making the money.

Digging deeper, Gilda felt an ancient need: as a young man he'd enjoyed the respect of a neighborhood friend after he'd saved him from a local gang. It was a pride he'd savored then almost as much as he reveled in the hunt now.

Gilda reignited that impulse—to seek approval for a good deed—with the last share of the blood she took, and then sealed the wound. She lifted him in her arms and carried him back out to the mouth of the cave. She left him in the brush as the sun began to round the horizon. When she turned back inside, the corridors were empty. She walked alone to Archelina's chamber.

She and Houston sat silently at the round table. Houston's gleaming sword rested at its center. He looked up as Gilda entered.

"He's gone?" he asked.

"Yes. On to a new career, I hope."

"Your gift is truly a wondrous one," Archelina said.

"I noticed you have a few tricks up your sleeve too," Gilda said. "I felt that I was paralyzed for a moment."

"Like most things, it's only energy. Understood. Channeled."

"Who taught you these arts?"

"In Iowa, my mother's people were healers. They battled the colonialists for generations. They were defeated often, but their spirit could never be taken away. To gather enough energy to hide is no great skill. Gathering enough energy to stand in the open, to hold onto your spirit, these are difficult things."

"How old are you?" Gilda asked.

Archelina laughed as Houston answered for her. "Not nearly as old as you, I bet."

"But well-preserved, I'm told," Archelina added.

Gilda flushed with embarrassment, as if Archelina had read her thoughts.

"I understand it's your custom to sleep during most of the day. Since it's almost dawn, I suggest we all retire for a while. Then you and Houston can set off refreshed."

Houston looked startled.

"You will be needing a guardian as you travel south to meet your family," Archelina continued. "Houston is a man to be trusted. He can be a friend."

"I have not settled yet on my direction or goal." Gilda felt annoyed at the presumption of knowledge when she'd made no decision herself.

"The message will come soon, and it will take you south to the caves of the Land of Enchantment. Then further south to meet the voices not of the past but of the future."

Again there was no room for contradiction. Gilda looked at Houston, who appeared pleased with Archelina's prognostication, and asked, "What do you say to this?"

"Archelina has great faith in me. I'm honored by that. But I'd only travel with you if it's what you wished." Houston looked into Gilda's eyes searching out her answer, then turned toward his sword, lifting it gently to return it to the shelf.

"I think our witch may be right."

Houston turned back to the table with a smile.

"I'd like to hear more of your stories, my friend. And maybe tell you some of my own. We'll start out at dusk."

Houston spread a blanket across the mat on a ledge below his sword. He sat up against the wall and wrapped the cover around him. He looked up at the painted stars and around the rough walls, believing he might not be seeing them for quite some time.

Gilda followed Archelina into the inner chamber. She unrolled her pallet, filled with her home soil, onto the sleeping platform which was built into the wall. She had never lain down with a mortal with whom she did not expect to share the blood. Everything about Archelina indicated she had no interest in the life Gilda might offer.

Still Gilda dropped her clothes easily beside the pallet and lay down. Archelina unwrapped the leggings from her ankles carefully and folded them on the floor along with the rest of her clothes. Her body was muscular, yet the skin had the looseness of age Gilda had so missed. Archelina folded Gilda into her arms under a feather cover and held her to her bosom, almost flat with the years. Gilda nestled against the witch as she might have against her own mother, or a lover. Her need was undefinable and consuming. She only knew the desire to be held. There was no single touch to remember, but a rolling persistence that fluttered across Gilda's skin and enflamed her core.

Archelina's strong hands massaged her arms and back, then touched her breasts, belly, and mouth tenderly. Gilda let her fingers caress the cool, dry folds of skin under the old woman's arm, and touch the tender skin where Archelina's breasts rested against her body. Their breathing rose to a humid pitch, synchronized, then became ragged. After some hours Gilda's breath slowed to almost a stop, and Archelina held her.

The darkness of the cave was complete, but both their bodies registered the changing day outside and the deliberate irregularity of Houston's breath as he sat watch in the outer chamber. Gilda was between sleeping and waking, her body in almost total stasis, yet she took in the thoughts and memories that wandered randomly through Archelina's mind. In them she found a sense of age she'd hungered for.

Gilda already knew what it meant to have those she loved die around her as time seemed to simply brush past her. But many other things could be taken in only through experiences that Gilda would never have: the ache that came from the inside of bones, the shadow of memory as faculties shed the needless details of the past, the sensation of nearing the end of your time. These were all things Archelina gave to Gilda as they lay in each other's arms.

In these hours Gilda saw how much of the future lies in the past. And how much was embedded in the single moment of the present. She, in turn, let Archelina experience the sense of being eternal—an open end of both familiarity and change. They lay together in wonder of each other's gifts and exchanged life in this way until dusk brought a new day, new roads, other magic. ✦